"Say my name, Elena," Rogan whispered

Elena felt the sting of tears behind her closed eyelids. "Blake," she murmured.

He brought her head against his chest. She could hear his heart beating beneath her ear, and a shudder went through her.

"And will you do as I tell you?" he asked then.

When she didn't answer, he cupped her head again and raised her face to his. "I hate you," she said in a broken whisper. "I hate you."

"Hate me all you like," he said, touching his tongue to her flesh. "I really don't give a damn. All I want is your word that you'll obey."

"Will you let me go if I say I will?"

His voice was thick. "Are you sure that's what you want?"

SANDRA MARTON says she's always believed in romance. She wrote her first love story when she was nine and fell madly in love at sixteen with the man who is her husband. Today they live on Long Island, mid-way between the glitter of Manhattan and the quiet beaches of the Atlantic. Sandra is delighted to be writing the kinds of stories she loves and even happier to find that her readers enjoy them, too.

Books by Sandra Marton

Don't miss any of our special offers. Write to us at the following address for information on our newest releases.

Harlequin Reader Service
901 Fuhrmann Blvd., P.O. Box 1397, Buffalo, NY 14240
Canadian address: P.O. Box 603,
Fort Erie, Ont. L2A 5X3

SANDRA MARTON

deal with the devil

Harlequin Books

TORONTO • NEW YORK • LONDON
AMSTERDAM • PARIS • SYDNEY • HAMBURG
STOCKHOLM • ATHENS • TOKYO • MILAN

Harlequin Presents first edition August 1989
ISBN 0-373-11194-0

Original hardcover edition published in 1988
by Mills & Boon Limited

Printed in U.S.A.

CHAPTER ONE

IT HAD been a mistake to come to the market. Elena knew it as soon as she stepped from the icy chill of the Cadillac Brougham into the fetid heat of the market-place in the centre of Santa Rosa. She could feel her white linen dress start wilting as the humidity and the smell reached out and wrapped her in unwanted embrace. She hesitated for a moment, the lacquered nails of one hand resting on the car's brightly waxed door, her green eyes narrowing as she looked around her. The square wasn't as she remembered it, she thought, gazing at the makeshift stalls. Where were all the laughing children? Where was the old man with the guitar who always sat on the kerb, singing love songs in the strange Spanish dialect of the hills?

'*Señorita?*'

Elena looked into the car. Her chauffeur's voice was properly polite, but there was no mistaking the look of concern in his dark eyes.

'If you have changed your mind,' he said, 'we can go back to the *hacienda*.'

It was the sound of his careful, accented English that made up her mind. She'd been back in Santa Rosa for a week, but everyone still treated her as if she were a tourist. She'd been born here, for goodness' sake. Had they all forgotten that? She was as much a San Felipian as anyone else—having an American mother had never changed that, nor had going to school in the States or even living there for the past three years. She was Elena Teresa Maria Consuelo Kelly-Esteban, and she was as much at home in this city and this country as she'd ever been.

She slammed the car door and smiled. 'Thank you, Juan,' she said, 'but I haven't changed my mind. I want to do some shopping, and I won't be needing you for a while. Please pick me up at the flower stalls in about an hour.'

'You will find few flowers for sale in the market, *señorita*,' the driver said. 'I have told you, it is not the same as you remember. Since the rebels...'

Elena waved her hand dismissively. 'They're in the mountains,' she said patiently. 'Not in the city.'

The man nodded. '*Sí*. But still, it is true, things are not as they were. People have come down from the hills. They are not the sort you are accustomed to. Please, *señorita,* let me take you back to your father's house. You do not belong in this place.'

For a moment, she almost agreed. The hot breeze blowing from the harbour had brought with it a whiff of dead fish and diesel oil, not the heavy fragrance of flowers and fruits she remembered. But then, nothing was quite as she remembered it. One of the reasons she'd insisted on going to the mid-week market was the hope that, if she got away from the rarefied atmosphere of Rancho Esteban and spent some time among the people of San Felipe, she'd feel less like a visitor and more like her father's daughter. Remembering that, Elena took a step away from the car.

'Go on, Juan,' she said gently. 'Stop being such an old woman. I'll be fine.'

'Your father will have my head if anything happens to you.'

'Nothing will, I promise.' A smile touched her lips. 'Do you still have a weakness for *tajadas*?'

For the first time all morning, Juan's broad face creased in a grin. 'Does the Río Bianco still flow to the sea?' he laughed.

Elena nodded. 'When you meet me at the flower stalls, I shall have a bag filled with chips for you. Now go and visit your sister. Be sure and give her my love. I'll see you in an hour.'

The driver sighed. 'She will be happy that you remember her, *señorita*.'

She smiled and patted the Cadillac's bumper. 'Off with you,' she said. 'And stop worrying. I can take care of myself. I'm not a child any more.'

She turned away before he could answer and blended quickly into the crowded market. It wasn't as colourful as she remembered it, but she'd been younger the last time she'd been here. Perhaps everything seemed different when you were eighteen years old and fresh from a Florida boarding-school. She'd been so happy to be home—she'd been away at school for five years, ever since her mother's death. But, after a few weeks, her father had insisted it was best if she returned north.

'I don't want to go, Papa,' she'd said. 'I love the ranch. And I've missed you terribly.'

Eduardo Esteban had put his arm around her and kissed her cheek. 'As I have missed you, Elena,' he'd said. 'And you shall come back soon, I promise. But...' His dark eyes had clouded suddenly. 'But things are unsettled in San Felipe. Until the future is more certain, I want you somewhere safe. It is for the best.'

She'd felt a cold sadness settle within her heart. How many times had she heard those words? It seemed as if there had always been a reason why she and her parents had to be apart. When she was younger, it had been her father's trips into the jungle to study the ruins of ancient civilisations. And then, when her mother had died, her

grief at the loss had been compounded by his decision
to send her away to school

Her American half had urged her to argue with him,
but the part of her that was obediently Spanish had won,
and Elena had finally nodded and done as he had asked.
She'd settled into a small apartment in Miami and taken
a job in an art gallery, only coming home twice for brief
visits. Until now. Until the rumours of unrest had begun
to flame across the Florida newspapers. Until she'd
begun to believe the headlines instead of her father's
carefully worded letters, assuring her that things were
fine, that nothing had changed.

The truth was that almost everything had changed. The
streets of the city were dirty. Most of the better stores
were boarded up and vacant. Even the market was different, just as Juan had warned it would be. There were
melons and squashes for sale as always, although not in
the jumbled profusion she remembered. But the stalls that
had sold sides of pork were shuttered. Only the one dealing
in live chickens was open, and it was doing lots of business.
The dark-eyed Indio women selling the silver and agate
jewellery so famous in San Felipe were gone, as were the
displays of striped blankets made of soft sheep's wool,
the woven baskets, and the clay pots.

And there were no tourists. That was the most obvious difference. Usually, they were everywhere in the
market, clutching their guidebooks and haggling with
the vendors in broken Spanish. In fact, Elena realised
uncomfortably, in her white dress and her dark leather
sandals, she looked the closest thing to a tourist in the
market. Of course, she wasn't one. It was just that she
felt so curiously out of place.

She paused beside a stand displaying hands of the tiny
red bananas her father had always loved. Perhaps the
sight of them at dinner would bring a smile to his gaunt

face, she thought, counting out a handful of coins in
exchange for the fruit. She smiled as she tucked the little
bananas into her oversized cotton shoulder-bag. Maybe
there would be papayas for sale, too. Those and the bananas and a dish of caramelised sugar . . .

'What in God's name are you doing here?'

Elena blinked and looked up. A man was standing in
front of her, barring her way.

'I beg your pardon,' she said coldly. 'Were you
speaking to me?'

'Do you see anybody else around here who'd be likely
to understand English?'

His voice was hard and unpleasant. She tilted her head
back, trying to see him more clearly, but the sun was
behind him, burning into her eyes and making it impossible to get a good look at him. What she saw,
however, she definitely did not like. He was tall and
broad-shouldered, and he smelled—she wrinkled her
nose delicately—he smelled of tobacco and male sweat.
It was not so much that it was an unpleasant combination; it was more that it was somehow threatening.
There was a battered, wide-brimmed hat pulled down
over his eyes—not that she could have seen them anyway,
she thought, looking at the dark, mirrored sunglasses
he wore. The bottom half of his face bristled with dark
stubble. And—yes, she thought, wrinkling her nose
again—of course, there was a dead cheroot clutched in
his teeth.

Elena's chin rose. 'Will you please step aside?'

'I asked you a question,' he said, putting his hands
on his hips. 'And you haven't answered it.'

This was ridiculous, she thought, staring at him. Who
did he think he was? Was he drunk? Her nose wrinkled
again. No, there was no trace of alcohol about him.

Crazy, then. Why not? It seemed anything was possible in Santa Rosa these days.

She shook her head in dismissal and started past him, but the man blocked her path again.

'You have no business in a place like this.'

'Get out of my way,' she said, anger flashing in her eyes. Still, he refused to move. She drew a deep breath. 'Did you hear me? I said, get out...'

'Slumming's a hell of a lot safer in Mexico than it is here, lady. Why don't you hop on a plane to Ixtapa?' Elena took a step back as he inched forward. 'It's made for people like you. You can rub shoulders with the peasants and bargain for cheap jewellery and have a hell of a time scaring yourself silly without risking your pretty little neck.'

'Look,' she said carefully, 'I'm sure you mean well, but...'

The man reached out and grasped her arm roughly, his fingers rasping through her thin silk dress to the skin beneath.

'You're coming with me,' he growled.

Elena's heart thumped. 'What?'

'You heard me. If you're so damned set on excitement, I'll...'

Don't let him frighten you, Elena told herself. This is broad daylight. You're in a public square.

'Do you see those soldiers across the square?' she asked him calmly. 'If you don't let go of me, I'm going to scream.'

He laughed softly. 'That should interest them, all right.'

'Perhaps you don't understand me,' she said carefully. 'If I were you, I'd think about what they'd do to a *gringo* who was molesting the daughter of Don Eduardo Esteban.'

The man's grip tightened. 'Is that supposed to impress me?'

She tilted her head back and looked into his face, watching her reflection in his mirrored lenses.

'I'll give you ten seconds to let go of me and step aside,' she said. 'One. Two. Three. Four...'

A muscle twitched at the corner of his mouth. She felt his fingers tighten for an instant and then his hand fell away.

'Right,' he said softly, and he took a step back. 'Have a good time, baby. Don't say I didn't warn you.'

She shouldered past him quickly, winding her way uphill and deeper into the market, her heart thudding erratically. Juan was right: coming here had been a mistake. Not that she'd ever admit it to him, she thought risking a glance over her shoulder and breathing a sigh of relief. The man was gone, vanished as quickly as he'd appeared. Well, so much for spending time among the people. Not that the man who'd accosted her had been San Felipian. His speech, his size, everything about him had told her he was an American.

She paused and looked behind her again. All she really wanted now was to head for the flower stalls and wait for Juan. She wondered if she should go back down the hill and retrace her steps. But the American might still be lurking about, waiting for her. Even if he'd only been bent on saving her in spite of herself, one run-in with him had been quite enough. She could still feel the imprint of his hand on her, still hear the harsh strength of his voice. No, she thought, it was far safer to go the long way round.

Elena's footsteps quickened. The market stalls thinned as they curved along the road leading up into the town's poorer streets. They would peter out eventually and be replaced by narrow, thick-smelling alleyways which would lead her back to the flower market. And then she'd find the stand that sold *tajadas* for Juan and she'd get into the Cadillac, lock the door behind her and forget all about the market.

She felt a hand brush lightly across the strap of her shoulder-bag. Elena turned quickly and found herself staring into a pair of dark eyes. The boy smiled and shrugged his shoulders, and she forced herself to nod in return. Her imagination was working overtime, she told herself as she hurried on. The boy hadn't bumped into her deliberately. He hadn't been interested in her purse…

She gasped as someone jostled her elbow. But it was only an old woman who smiled and murmured an apology.

'*Dispénseme, señorita.* Excuse me.'

'My fault,' Elena said with a strained smile.

She was half-way down an alley now, and the stalls were gone. The shoppers were gone, too. The graffiti-scarred walls, mottled in shadow, echoed her footsteps. A shiver of fear chilled the nape of her neck. Perhaps she ought to go back the way she'd come. Perhaps…

The alley narrowed ahead, partially blocked by a peddler's cart. A man leaned against it and Elena brushed against him as she passed.

'*Dispénseme,*' she said. But there was no answering voice, no equally polite apology. Instead, she felt a hand move quickly across her hip, the touch slowing on her buttocks. 'Hey,' she said, spinning around angrily, 'what are you…'

The man who had been leaning against the cart had been silently joined by another, and their eyes were on her, moving across her breasts and her hips like snakes slithering across the grass. She flushed and turned away at their lewd laughter. The alley stretched on interminably, shadowy and narrow, its shuttered windows and closed doorways seeming like sightless eyes and sealed mouths that would remain frighteningly indifferent to all pleas for help. A muffled sound caught in her throat and her heart began to pound.

OK, she thought, moving on and quickening her pace, it was time to get out of here. More than 'things' had changed in San Felipe. People had changed, too. Even the possibility of a stranger looking at a woman as those two had just looked at her would have been out of the question in the past. Santa Rosa was a small city in a small country, but it had been a good place to live. Its citizens had been poor, but everyone, especially women, had been treated with honour. You never had to worry about anyone trying to...

An arm snaked around her shoulders and pulled her into a loose embrace. Hot, beery breath floated into her face.

'You need a man, baby.'

Elena's head snapped back and she pushed free of the encircling arm, which slipped to her waist and held her. A youth in filthy clothing stood beside her, a foolish grin on his pock-marked face.

'Let go of me,' she said quietly.

His grin widened, revealing blackened teeth and swollen gums. 'Hey, baby,' he repeated in thickly accented English, 'wanna...?'

Don't let him frighten you, she told herself, forcing her eyes to meet his. He's just trying to be macho.

'Let go of me,' she said again, this time in rapid Spanish. 'Take your hand off me at once!'

'Baby, baby, I need you,' a second male voice whispered, and Elena's head swivelled as an arm wound around her shoulders.

And then, as she stared into the slack-jawed faces, one nodded almost imperceptibly to the other, and they began to drag her along between them. She dug her san-dalled feet into the dirt street, but it was useless. She was being led further into the alley. And there was no one watching, no one looking, no one to see what became of her. This was ridiculous, she thought angrily. Things like this just didn't happen, not in broad daylight. Not here.

'Listen,' she said in a final appeal to their sense of decency, 'you'd better let go of me before you get into trouble. You two...'

The boy on her left laughed. 'You love it, baby,' he whispered, leaning towards her. Elena drew away from his rank breath as he bent towards her, and his kiss landed wetly on the corner of her mouth. She grimaced as a trickle of saliva threaded across her cheek.

'Stop it,' she said, and she began to struggle in des-peration. 'Damn you, stop it!'

The boy to her right cupped his hand across her mouth and said something in a low, coarse whisper. He spoke in a dialect unfamiliar to her, but its meaning was clear. His companion laughed as Elena moaned softly against her captor's filthy hand.

'*Sí,*' he said, and his embrace tightened until only her toes were touching the dusty ground. They had turned down another alley now; the smell of urine and beer filled her nose and throat and made her gag.

'You need it, baby,' the boy whispered, his voice husky with urgency, and suddenly she was slammed back against a wall and both boys were standing in front of her, grinning drunkenly.

Their mothers would kill them if they knew what they were up to, Elena thought crazily, staring at the dirty faces of her assailants. Neither one looked old enough to shave. No, she told herself, it was impossible.

And then it didn't matter who they were or how young they seemed. Their hot breath was on her face and neck and their hands were at her breasts and buttocks, pulling at her clothing, grasping and hurting. Elena kicked out blindly and one of her attackers gave a muffled curse. An arm encircled her throat and she gasped for breath.

'No!' she cried, but her voice was only a whisper, and her assailants laughed.

'Puta,' one of them said in her ear, his body pressing against hers.

Suddenly, she was free of his weight. She heard him cry out, heard the other boy's voice in answering echo, and her eyes opened wide.

The American, the man who had confronted her earlier, was holding her assailants by the scruff of their necks, shaking them as if they were sacks of dirty laundry. He tossed one of them aside and the boy scurried to his feet and raced away without a backward glance. The other—the one who had pressed his wet mouth to her face—slammed his fist into the man's face. Elena heard the crack of flesh against bone, saw the man's head snap back, and then the man moved with the speed of a leopard and the boy was on the ground, writhing in the mud, clutching his stomach while the man bent over him.

'Don't,' she whispered, clutching at his arm. 'Please— you'll kill him.'

'The little bastard deserves killing,' the man growled, but he straightened up and the boy scrambled to his feet and ran off, his arms wrapped around his middle. 'Go on,' the man yelled. 'If I see you again, you're dead. Rotten scum,' he muttered, turning towards Elena. 'What hope is there for anybody if . . . Hey,' he said urgently, 'hey, don't pass out on me now!'

'I'm not going to do that,' Elena said in a breathy whisper, but even as she spoke, she felt herself sagging towards him. His arms closed tightly around her.

'All right,' he said softly, 'take it easy. You're fine now. Come on, take a deep breath. That's it. And another.'

He cupped the back of her head and brought her face to his chest. Elena closed her eyes and buried her nose in his shirt, drinking in the smell of tobacco and sweat as if it were nectar, hearing his heartbeat thud strong and steady beneath her ear, knowing somehow that she was safe within his embrace. She took one long, shuddering breath and then another.

'They didn't . . . you're OK, aren't you?'

Elena nodded. 'Yes,' she said finally, 'yes, I'm fine. They didn't...they just frightened me. Although, if you hadn't come along . . .'

Suddenly, he thrust her from him, holding her at arm's length, staring angrily into her face. He had taken off his sunglasses, she noticed. His eyes—blue, and cold as ice—burned into hers.

'Yes,' he said, 'exactly. That's what I tried to tell you before, but you weren't having any part of it, were you Miss Esteban?'

'How . . . how do you know my name?' she whispered.

His mouth twisted. 'You told it to me,' he said roughly. 'You rubbed my nose in it, to be accurate. Don't you remember?'

She nodded. 'I thought you were . . . Where did you come from? Were you following me?'

His hands fell to his sides. 'Don't flatter yourself. There's a black market up the next street—I heard they had Cuban cigars. I got here just in time to see our two little friends hustling you off for some fun and games.'

A dark flush covered Elena's cheeks. 'They were only boys,' she said defensively. 'I can't believe...'

'How much more proof do you want?' he asked sharply, his eyes sliding from her pale face to her breasts.

She glanced down at herself, the flush darkening as she realised that the top buttons of her dress had come undone. Her gaze met his again, and something she saw in the midnight-blue depths of his eyes made her uneasy. Quickly, she grasped the gaping neckline and pulled it together.

'Thank you for your help,' she said. 'Now, if you'd just step aside...'

His eyebrows rose. 'Step aside?'

Elena nodded. 'So I can get past you,' she said. 'My chauffeur is waiting for me at the bottom of the hill and...'

'And you're going to walk down there and meet him.'

She nodded again. His tone was pleasant, but there was something in the sudden narrowing of his eyes that made her take a step back.

'Yes,' she said, 'that's right. Thank you again, Mr... Mr...'

He threw his hands in the air. 'For Christ's sake,' he said angrily, 'here we go again! What's the matter with you, Miss Esteban? Haven't you learned a damned thing?' She flinched as he moved towards her. 'Terrific,' he snarled. 'You're afraid of me, not the bastards who almost raped you! I'm only the man who saved your neck.'

'No, that's not it,' she said quickly. 'You don't understand.'

But how could he? she thought, looking into his face. The attempted rape had frightened her. But the pain of seeing what had happened to the place she'd always thought of as home was a wound she knew would never

heal. The part of her that was American was angry—
but the part that was San Felipian was busily denying
the terrible truth even as it unfolded all around her.

The man was staring at her, lines of disbelief etched
into his face. It was a handsome face, she thought suddenly, if you liked the hard as steel type. She certainly
didn't—but he had been kind to her. More than kind.
And he was entitled to some kind of an explanation.

'It's not that I'm ungrateful,' she began, and suddenly tears welled in her eyes.

A shadow flickered across his face. 'Oh, for God's
sake,' he said furiously, and then he grasped her
shoulders and pulled her towards him. 'Don't cry,
dammit,' he said gruffly. 'It's all over now.'

But there was no way she could stop the silent flow
of tears that dampened his shirt. His hands moved softly
on her back, their motion soothing and comforting, and
finally Elena drew a ragged breath.

'I'm sorry,' she whispered, moving back against his
encircling arms and looking up at him. 'I . . . I guess I'm
more upset than I realised. You see, I came back to San
Felipe a week ago, and nothing is the way it used to be.
I can't seem to get used to all the changes.'

He sighed deeply. 'Welcome to the real world, Miss
Esteban. You can't go home again, not really. Didn't
anyone ever tell you that?'

'Yes, but you see, I grew up here. And it was so different . . .' Her words drifted into silence as she looked
at him. A thin beading of scarlet welled on his lip.
'You're hurt,' she said quickly.

He touched his tongue to the cut. 'It's nothing. The
little s.o.b. got lucky, that's all.' A grin spread across
his face. 'Believe me, he'll remember me a lot longer
than I'll remember him.'

'Yes, but it's all my fault, Mr . . . Mr . . .'

His arms dropped to his sides. 'Rogan,' he said. 'Blake Rogan. And you're damned right it's your fault.' Colour washed her cheeks again. Her apology had been automatic; she hadn't expected his easy and whole-hearted agreement. 'If you'd listened to me the first time, if you'd let me find you a taxi, put you into it and send you home...'

Elena blinked. 'Is that what you wanted to do?'

Rogan's eyes narrowed. 'What did you think I wanted to do, Miss Esteban?'

She swallowed. 'Well, I...I mean you...you said if I...if I wanted some excitement, you'd...you'd...'

Rogan swore softly. 'I'll be damned! There I was, trying to keep you out of trouble, and you thought I was...' He shook his head. 'Hell, you were quick enough to make excuses for those punks who jumped you.'

Elena shook her head. She wanted to tell him it wasn't like that, that she knew her assailants would have hurt her if he hadn't come along, that only her own emotional memories of San Felipe made her defend them, but Rogan was moving towards her again, his eyes narrowed.

'Where have you been for the last few years?' he murmured. 'In a convent?'

'No,' she said nervously, remembering her very proper boarding-school, 'not exactly, but...' She took a final, stumbling step backward and her shoulders hit the wall. 'Look, Mr Rogan, I'm sorry if I misjudged you earlier. And I really am very grateful...'

Rogan smiled. 'You didn't misjudge me,' he said softly. 'Not entirely.' Elena watched, wide-eyed, as his hand reached towards her. His fingers touched her cheek, lingering against the soft sweep of her jaw. 'You're a very beautiful woman, Miss Esteban. And there are times that can be dangerous as hell. Someone should have explained that to you.'

Elena's breath quickened. His fingers were hard, the pads rough as they stroked her skin, but his touch was gentle. She felt his hand curving around her jaw.

'No one has to explain anything to me, Mr Rogan. I understand. I'm not a fool. But I've always been safe here...'

His hand cupped the back of her head. 'You're not any more,' he growled. 'Don't you understand that yet?'

'Let go of me, please,' she said carefully.

'You're not really a San Felipian, are you? You look American, you sound American...'

His fingers were threading into the dark silk of her hair. She could feel the warmth of his breath on her face. For some reason, her heart was thudding like a trip-hammer.

'What I am is none of your business, Mr Rogan. And I'd appreciate it if you'd let go of me.'

Rogan leaned towards her. 'Get the hell out of San Felipe, Miss Esteban. Go back to wherever it is you came from before it's too late.'

'I can take care of myself, Mr Rogan. This is my country. I don't need any advice from you.'

She drew in her breath as his fingers caught tightly in her hair. 'You damned well need it from somebody,' he said fiercely. 'And it might as well be me.'

His free arm swept around her and suddenly his mouth covered hers in a hard kiss. Elena whimpered and slammed her hands against his chest, but Rogan only pulled her more closely against him until she could feel the full length of his body pressing against hers. And then, as quickly as it had begun, the kiss ended. Rogan's hands grasped her shoulders and he thrust her from him.

'Do you understand now?' he demanded, his eyes locked with hers. 'You're a woman in a place that's going to bust wide open any day now. Anything can happen to you.'

'No,' Elena whispered, 'no, it's not true.'

But it was. She knew it; she had known it from the moment she'd returned home. The reality she'd been denying for days engulfed her. Tears filled her eyes again, and with sudden, ridiculous clarity she realised that she hadn't cried this much since her mother's death.

Rogan's eyes darkened. 'Hell,' he said gruffly, 'don't do that. I didn't mean to make you cry.'

'It's all right,' she whispered, 'I . . .'

But it wasn't all right. He watched as tears began to trickle down her cheeks, and then he took a step forward and his arms encircled her. Their eyes met; his head bent slowly towards hers.

Elena's heart raced as his mouth touched hers again. She started to struggle against him, but a slow warmth began spreading through her as she felt the firm pressure of his lips on hers. She sighed, her lashes falling against her cheeks, and Rogan made a sound in the back of his throat as he gathered her more closely against him. His kiss hardened, became more demanding, and her lips parted willingly beneath the gentle pressure. She felt the scalding touch of his tongue, tasted the sweetness of his mouth—and then, suddenly, his hands were on her shoulders and he was pushing her away from him.

Her eyes flew open. His face was dark with rage, and she stumbled back a step. Rogan stared at her for what seemed an eternity, and then he took a ragged breath.

'If I ever see you in the streets alone again,' he said hoarsely, 'you'll regret it.' His eyes narrowed to dangerous slits. 'Do you understand?'

No, she thought, looking at him, no, I don't understand any of what just happened to me... But she nodded instead.

'Yes,' she whispered, touching her hand lightly to her mouth. She looked at her finger; it was smeared with crimson. His blood, she thought dizzily. Rogan's blood. 'Yes,' she said again, 'I understand.'

He nodded. 'I sure as hell hope so. Because...'

'Señorita?'

Elena spun around. 'Juan,' she said softly, closing her eyes with relief. 'How... how did you find me?'

Her chauffeur stood at the head of the alley, looking from her to Blake Rogan.

'Are you all right, *señorita*? I waited at the flower stalls, but when you did not come, I decided to look for you myself.'

'I'm fine,' she said quickly, knowing how she must look, her dress torn, her mouth smeared with blood, and she forced a smile to her face. 'Really, Juan, I'm all right. Thanks to this gentleman here. Perhaps we can offer him a lift...'

She turned quickly, but somehow it came as no great surprise to see the alley looming dark and empty beyond her.

Blake Rogan had vanished.

CHAPTER TWO

SUNSET in Santa Rosa had always been Elena's favourite time of day. The hot red disc that was the sun seemed to balance precariously over the mountains that ringed the city, bleeding crimson flame on the rugged peaks while night gathered its forces. Then, with breathtaking suddenness, it would fall and allow everything to be cloaked in indigo velvet.

But on this, the night of her twenty-first birthday, not even the fierce beauty of the setting sun was enough to dispel her uneasiness. Tension in the city had grown. There were ugly rumours of danger on the streets and roads, and Elena's father had refused to let her leave the ranch since that day at the market, that day two weeks ago when Blake Rogan had kissed her...

Elena switched on the bedside lamp and undid the towel from her hair. She hadn't told her father about that part of it, of course. Juan had told him all he knew of the incident, that the American had saved her from rape, perhaps even from death, and there had been no reason for her to add anything more. Her father's only regret was that he hadn't been able to thank her saviour personally. She wondered what he'd say if he knew that Rogan had forced his kiss upon her.

She crossed the room swiftly and opened the wardrobe door. Actually, she knew what he'd say. There was enough old-fashioned Spanish blood in Eduardo Esteban's veins so that he'd fly into a rage. In her father's world, men didn't take advantage of women. Obviously, in Blake Rogan's world, you took what you wanted when you wanted it. But, if her father chose to think of him as a hero, let him. What harm was there in that? Besides, for some reason that she preferred not to explore, she wanted the knowledge of Rogan's kiss to be hers and hers alone.

It wasn't as if she would ever see him again, she reminded herself as she peered into the wardrobe. A man like that didn't move in the same circles as the Estebans. Americans like Rogan were the sort who drifted ever southward, searching for something that didn't exist. Central America was only a stopover for that kind of adventurer.

She took a green silk dress from its hanger and pulled it over her head. Certainly, she had no wish to see the man again. There wasn't even any logical reason to think of him as often as she did—unless it was because he'd saved her from her own foolishness. Yes, she thought, holding the dress against herself, yes, that was the reason. Of course it was.

She dropped her robe to the floor and slipped the dress over her head. It was a bit tight across the breasts and hips, and she looked at herself critically in the full-length mirror on the back of the wardrobe door. Too snug, she thought wryly. The dress had a rounded neckline and a softly draped skirt. It had been fine when she'd bought it two years before, during her last visit home. But she'd been nineteen then, she reminded herself with a frown as she peered into the mirror. Her breasts hadn't been quite as full and her hips hadn't been as gently rounded. The dress had been fitted for a girl, and somehow, during the intervening years, she'd grown into a woman.

There was nothing else in the wardrobe that would do. All her old dresses were there, but none of them would fit any better than this. She'd brought clothes with her, of course, but nothing festive. It had never occurred to her that there'd be an occasion for a party dress, not after all the rumours she'd heard about what was happening in San Felipe. But she hadn't counted on her father's stubbornness.

'Are you saying we should not celebrate my only child's twenty-first birthday?' Eduardo Esteban had demanded when she'd gently tried to turn aside his plans. 'Nonsense, *querida*. Of course we shall have a party. A fine one!'

'Yes, but with things the way they are, Papa...'

'Don't worry about that, *querida*. There is still wine in the cellar—even some champagne. And you know that Maria works magic in the kitchen.' He had smiled and put his arm around Elena's waist. 'Would you deny an old man his pleasure?'

And she had smiled and put her head on his shoulder. 'You're not an old man, Papa,' she'd said softly.

She bent now and picked out a pair of black silk sandals. No, she thought, he wasn't old. But he looked as if he were. Lines and shadows had appeared in her father's face during the past days. He was worried. She knew it, even though he denied it. Just last night, at dinner, he'd told her he was going to arrange for her flight back to Miami.

'Will you come with me?' she'd asked quickly.

Esteban had shaken his head. 'I must stay, *querida*. I will be safe, I assure you. All this nonsense will be over soon.'

'I won't leave you. I'll stay with you, Papa.'

Her father's eyes flashed. 'You will do as I tell you, Elena. It's...'

'...for the best,' she said. 'I know.'

Their eyes met across the table; finally, she'd looked away. She wasn't a child to be sent away quietly any more, she'd thought, but there was no sense in forcing an argument. She would do what she had to do, when and if the time came. Until then, she'd do what she could to make her father happy. And that meant she'd smile and try her best to enjoy the party tonight.

'This is an important occasion, Elena,' he'd said. 'You must tell me who you wish to invite.'

The answer had come to her without any warning. 'Blake Rogan,' she'd said immediately. Her father's eyebrows rose and colour had washed into her cheeks. 'I just thought it might be a way to thank him for his kindness,' she'd said quickly.'

'A good idea, Elena. If we can locate your Mr Rogan, we shall invite him.'

She'd felt the heat in her cheeks. 'He's not *my* Mr Rogan, Papa,' she'd said coolly. 'You're the one who keeps talking about thanking the man. But now that I think of it, I doubt if it's a good idea. Anyway, you'd never be able to find him.'

Elena blinked her eyes and stared into the mirror. What on earth had made her think of inviting Blake Rogan tonight? Good manners? She smiled at herself as she ran her comb through her hair. Yes, of course. That was it. Her mother had taught her to do the proper thing, as had an endless succession of housekeepers and, of course, so had the teachers at boarding-school. They had all taught her well. She never used the wrong fork or forgot to write a thank-you note. Her whole existence had been 'proper'. Maybe that was why Rogan's lean, muscled body had felt so exciting against hers. Maybe that was why she could still remember the sweet hardness of his kiss.

There was a light tap at the bedroom door. '*Querida?* May I come in?'

Elena touched her hands to her pink cheeks and swallowed hard. 'Yes, of course,' she said after a pause, 'come in, Papa.' She flung the door open and smiled. 'How do I look?' she asked, twirling before him.

'You look lovely, *querida*. You're the image of your mother.'

'That's the nicest compliment you could have given me,' she said, kissing his cheek. 'Thank you, Papa.'

Eduardo Esteban's smile faded. 'Elena,' he said slowly, 'I've been thinking of what we discussed at dinner last night.'

'You've changed your mind about my leaving? Oh, I'm so glad to hear it. I...'

'I've decided to make arrangements for your departure, Elena. You will fly home next week.'

'No,' she said quickly, 'I won't. I'm not going without you, Papa.'

Her father sighed. 'You not only look like your mother, you sound like her. Don't be stubborn, child. I only want what's best for you.'

'And I want the same thing for you, Papa. If you think it's unsafe for me to stay here, then it's time for you to leave, too.'

'We've been all through this, Elena. This ranch belonged to my father and my father's father. I will never just walk away from it. Besides, there are different dangers for a young woman than there are for me. You know that. If your Mr Rogan hadn't come along in time...'

Elena clucked her tongue. 'For the last time, Papa, he's not *my* Mr Rogan. I keep telling you that. You make him sound like a saint.'

Her father smiled. 'Not a saint, Elena.'

'Papa, about this Mr Rogan of yours...'

Her father laughed. 'He's not *my* Mr Rogan, either, *querida*.'

Elena chuckled softly. 'OK, I deserved that. But...'

'Enough talk for tonight, Elena.' Her father offered her his arm and she took it. 'It's time to join our guests and celebrate your birthday.'

She smiled as they stepped on to the balcony that ran the length of the second floor.

'I can't believe you'd make a party now, Papa,' she said as the sound of laughter and music drifted up the wide stairway.

Later, she would remember the darkness in her father's eyes as he bent and kissed her cheek.

'Perhaps that's the very reason I did it, *querida*,' he said softly, and before she could answer, he tucked her hand into the crook of his arm and began to lead her down the steps.

Her father had outdone himself, Elena thought an hour later as she drifted from room to room. There was tinned pâté and caviar, dredged from who knew what hidden source. And there were cheeses and fresh breads, even an enormous platter of *paella*—clams and chicken and sausage served over rice. There was red wine and white wine and even bottles of cool, dark beer imported from Mexico—all things that were in short supply in San Felipe lately. Elena suspected he'd depleted the wine cellar and the pantry. But no one seemed to care.

What on earth was wrong with her? she thought, shaking her head. This was her birthday party, and here she was, walking around with a phoney smile plastered to her face, feeling as depressed as if she were at a funeral. No, she thought, no that wasn't really it at all. She felt as if she were in Rome the night before the barbarians sacked it. Everyone was eating and drinking and having a wonderful time. But there was something artificial about all the merriment, as if people knew the end was coming and were determined to have one last fling.

Her face ached from the effort it took to keep smiling, and her ears rang with the sound of the forced laughter. Even the music was too loud; someone had put a stack of records on the phonograph and no matter how many times she turned down the volume, it was always turned up again within minutes. If this was a birthday party, it was like none she'd ever attended. And she hadn't seen her father in more than an hour. She'd gone looking for him earlier, but he was nowhere to be seen. She'd searched out Juan and asked him if he knew where her father was.

'Your father is in his study, *señorita*,' he'd said.

Again, that chill hand had clutched at her. 'Is he ill?'

The chauffeur had shaken his head. 'No, no, he is fine, *señorita*. It is a matter of business. He is meeting with someone.'

'Business? In the middle of all this?'

Juan's dark, Indio face had been impassive. He'd shrugged, and finally she'd given up and drifted off again, moving from group to group, chatting and laughing until she couldn't keep up the pretence any longer. Now she stood in a corner, a glass of watered-down wine in her hand, a cool smile on her lips, watching the partygoers carry on. When she realised that she felt more like an observer than a participant, she decided it was time to go outside for a breath of fresh air.

She wound her way through the crowded house until she reached the double doors that led to the patio. She opened them and slipped outside, leaning back against them and sighing with relief as they swung closed. The old, solid oak doors muffled the music as effectively as if she'd pulled the phonograph cord from the wall. The night air was cool; for a second, she thought of going back inside for a scarf, but then she remembered the noise and the raucous laughter, and she decided it was better to be chilled than to be inundated with all that unreal hilarity again, and she wrapped her arms around herself and took a few cautious steps forward.

She could see nothing. The night was deep and dark; a crescent moon rode high in the black sky, but it cast little light on the flagstone patio. Usually, the patio was lit at night. And, on the night of a party, the regular electric lights were always augmented with festive paper lanterns, both here and in the flower garden to the side of the house. But there were no lights at all tonight. Her father had tried to explain the darkness by making a joke about Santa Rosa's power company.

'You know how it is, Elena,' he'd said. 'We don't want to tempt fate by putting a strain on the system.'

She'd let him think she believed that, but she'd overheard Juan saying that lights might only make the house a target. Although it was a frightening possibility, it was a more reasonable one than her father's excuse.

An owl called in the darkness and Elena shuddered. Her eyes widened, as if trying to see into the blackness beyond the patio. Perhaps coming out here hadn't been such a good idea, she thought. She'd never been afraid of the dark, and certainly she'd never been afraid of the ranch, but tonight she felt like a stranger here. Nothing seemed familiar, not the shadowed outlines of the trees and bushes beyond the patio, nor the sigh of the breeze that brought the spicy scent of herbs and the sweetness of the flowers drifting to her from the garden. In fact, those scents were overshadowed by something else. Tobacco smoke, she thought, and her heart skipped a beat. Yes, there it was. She could just make out the red glow of a cigarette.

'Good evening.'

The voice was male, soft and vaguely familiar. A neighbour? Or perhaps it was one of her father's friends. But the man had spoken to her in English—in American, to be specific. She could tell that by the accent...

Elena's heartbeat quickened. 'Rogan?' she whispered.

A shadowy form moved in the darkness. 'At your service, *señorita*,' he said. 'We meet again, it seems.'

Was she crazy, or was there a thread of laughter in his voice? 'What are you doing here, Rogan?' she asked after a pause.

'Enjoying one of your father's Cuban cigars,' he said, and now she could just make out his outline against the night sky. The red tip glowed more brightly for an instant. 'He apparently has a better source than I have. I haven't been able to buy anything this good in years.'

'Did my father invite you here, Mr Rogan?'

'Would you prefer to think I gatecrashed, Miss Esteban?'

There *was* laughter in his voice. She could hear it clearly now, and it infuriated her. In fact, the man's presence infuriated her. What on earth was he doing here?

'I asked you a simple question,' she said tersely. 'Did my father invite you here?'

Rogan stepped forward. In the faint wash of moonlight, he seemed even taller and more broad-shouldered than he had that day at the market place.

'*You* invited me, Elena,' he said softly.

She felt her cheeks flame, and she was grateful for the darkness which must be shielding her from his eyes as it was shielding him from hers.

'I did no such thing, Mr Rogan,' she said quickly.

He laughed softly. 'Are you calling your father a liar?'

'No, of course not...'

'He told me he was inviting me at your specific request.'

She closed her eyes as she remembered the impetuous words she'd spoken the week before.

'My father misunderstood me,' she lied. 'He had been saying he wanted to thank you for helping me that day at the market, and I merely suggested it was too bad he didn't know your whereabouts, that if he did, he could invite you to this party by way of expressing his gratitude. There was nothing personal in it...'

'Your cordiality is overwhelming,' he said, and she felt herself blush again.

'I'm not trying to be impolite, Mr Rogan. I merely wanted to set things straight between us. I wouldn't want you to think...'

'You didn't tell him everything that happened that day, Elena.'

The red glow that was the tip of the cigar arced through the darkness like a meteor and landed on the patio. Elena watched as it smouldered hotly, and then Rogan's foot crushed it into blackness.

'I don't know what that's supposed to mean,' she said quickly. 'I always tell him everything. I...'

She drew back as Rogan took a step forward. He looked nothing like the man she'd met in Santa Rosa. His dark hair was combed back neatly, although she could see that it was a little long, as if it hadn't been trimmed in a while. It curled lightly over his shirt collar. A white shirt, she realised, worn with a tie, beneath a dark, well-fitted suit. The bristly beard was gone. Only his cold blue eyes were exactly as she remembered them.

'Surely, not everything,' he said softly.

Elena's eyes met his. 'I...I... What did you say?'

Rogan grinned. 'I said, surely you don't tell your father everything. You must have some secrets you want to keep.'

Elena swallowed drily. 'Mr Rogan...'

He grinned again. 'Rogue.'

'I'm sure the name is appropriate, Mr Rogan...'

'It's what my friends call me.'

'We're not friends, Mr Rogan. We...'

He frowned. 'But we're not strangers, are we, Elena? Not after what we've shared.'

Elena stared into his eyes and then she turned on her heel and started towards the house.

'Goodnight, Mr Rogan. I'll tell my father you had to leave without saying goodbye.'

She gasped as his hands bit into her shoulders. 'You're not afraid of me, are you, Elena?'

Her eyes closed as she stiffened in his grasp. 'I won't dignify that with a response, Mr Rogan. I'll simply ask you to let go of me and...'

'I seem to remember saving your neck the last time we met. Now you're acting as if I was the one who'd tried to hurt you.'

Elena's eyes opened. 'Mr Rogan, you have an amazingly selective memory. No, you didn't try to hurt me. But you...you... You forced yourself on me, and...'

His laughter was quick and deep. 'Forced myself on you?' Rogan's fingers tightened as he turned her slowly towards him. 'That's a lovely, old-fashioned phrase, *señorita*, but it doesn't apply to what happened that day. Those snot-nosed little bastards were trying to force themselves on you, not me.'

Elena's chin lifted. 'Did you think I'd forgotten that you kissed me?' she demanded.

A smile lifted the corners of his mouth. 'Yes,' he said softly, 'actually, I was beginning to think just that. I mean, you didn't tell your father about it. He'd hardly have been so ... eager to do business with me if he knew how you'd melted in my arms.'

'Oh, for heaven's sake!' she snapped, trying unsuccessfully to pull free of his grasp. 'I did no such thing. I ... What are you doing, Mr Rogan?'

'Refreshing your memory,' he said softly, slipping his arms around her.

He drew her closer to him, and Elena put her hands flat against his chest. 'Let go of me,' she said. 'If you don't, I'll ...'

'You'll what?' His voice was a husky murmur, and she could feel his warm breath against her face. 'Your father told me this was your twenty-first birthday. In my world, that means you're a woman, Elena.' A shudder ran through her as she felt the light brush of his mouth on her earlobe. 'You were woman enough when I kissed you in the market-place.'

A slow, sweet lethargy was spreading along her spine and through her limbs. Rogan's hands were slipping along her back. She could feel the heat of his palms and fingers through the thin silk dress. Her hands were still pressed against his chest, and she could feel the steady thud of his heart beneath them, but he was gathering her closer against him, bringing her into the hard warmth of his body.

'Listen,' he said softly. 'Someone's playing the guitar. Do you hear it?'

Elena's eyes closed. Yes, she thought as the faint strains drifted towards her, yes, she could hear it now. It was coming from the bunkhouse down by the corral. One of the *rancheros* was playing a soft, sad melody on a Spanish guitar.

'*Mi corazon,*' Rogan said, whispering the familiar words in her ear, '*mi amor, siempre juntitos*... My heart, my love, always together...'

She took a deep breath and then another. 'Mr Rogan,' she said, 'you can't...'

He laughed softly. 'Can't I?'

She wanted to push him from her, to slap his face, to tell him he was an impudent bastard. But instead, she was melting as she had before, her eyes closing expectantly, her mouth parting as his head bent towards her. And then, suddenly, the doors to the house opened, and music and light blasted apart the dream world his soft words and touch had created.

'Let go of me, Rogan,' Elena demanded.

But he already had. She felt his arms drop away from her and his hands grasped her shoulders as he took a step back.

'Your wish is my command, *señorita*,' he said, his voice thick with insolence.

'You just wait until I tell my father,' she said breathlessly. 'He'll have you thrown out of here. He'll have you tossed out of the country. He...'

'Good evening, Mr Rogan.'

Elena blinked in surprise. 'Papa?' she asked softly.

Eduardo Esteban smiled. 'I see you and Mr Rogan found each other without my help, Elena. I hoped you would; I didn't want to spoil the surprise.'

'The surprise?' she repeated flatly, looking from her father to Rogan.

'Mr Rogan is your birthday present, *querida*. You said you wished him to be present at your party, and here he is.'

She watched incredulously as her father clapped Rogan on the back. Both men were smiling, but Rogan's smile seemed strained. Not as strained as mine, she thought suddenly, as she forced her lips to curve upward.

'Well,' she said finally, and then she cleared her throat. 'Well, that was very thoughtful of you, Papa. And now, if you'll both excuse me . . .'

'Elena.'

She paused half-way across the patio and waited for her father to tell her she was being rude. But when he spoke again, it was to Blake Rogan.

'Has it gone as I said it would, Mr Rogan?'

Elena turned towards the two men and frowned. 'What are you talking about, Papa? Has *what* gone as you said?'

Her father shrugged. 'Mr Rogan and I had a discussion earlier this evening. He had some questions and I suggested he seek the answers himself.'

'Questions?' She looked from one man to the other, but neither looked at her. Instead, Rogan scowled.

'She flirts with danger,' he said flatly, staring at Eduardo Esteban. 'I don't think she'd recognise trouble if it bit her on the nose.'

Elena gasped. 'Are you talking about me, Mr Rogan? Papa, did you hear what he said? He . . .'

Her father waved a dismissive hand in her direction. 'That may be true, Mr Rogan. But my daughter was brought up to be obedient. She will do as she is told.'

Rogan barely glanced at her. 'She's not as obedient as you think, Esteban. She'll do what I tell her to do, though. My methods aren't the same as yours, but they've worked so far.'

Elena felt a flood of heat start at her toes and race towards her face.

'You . . . you son of a bitch,' she whispered. 'You bastard. You . . .'

Eduardo Esteban shrugged his shoulders. 'She has, as I have already told you, spent most of her life in the United States. I apologise for her bad manners, Mr Rogan. But I think, under the circumstances, you would rather she have spirit than not, don't you agree?'

'I suppose so. But if I go through with this, I sure as hell don't want her deciding to be liberated at the wrong moment.'

Elena's head swivelled from one man to the other as if she were at some insane tennis match. They were talking about her as if she were some kind of commodity that one was trying to sell the other and the other didn't want to buy. None of it made any sense, but no matter how many times she tried to interrupt, neither man paid her the slightest attention. Finally, she stepped between them and held up her hands.

'Stop it!' she demanded furiously. 'Someone had better tell me what's going on around here. Have you lost your mind, Papa? You're allowing this man to... to discuss me, as if I were up for sale or for rent...'

Her father stepped forward and put his arm around her shoulders. 'Forgive me, *querida*. I should explain, of course. You see, Mr Rogan may be able to help me get you out of the country, and...'

Relief flooded her senses. 'For goodness' sake, Papa,' she said with a quick smile, 'is that what this is all about? I'm not going. I already told you that.'

Eduardo Esteban nodded. 'Yes, I know. But...'

'Besides, you told me you I was flying home next week. I thought that meant you'd bought me a plane ticket.'

'I have, *querida*. But...'

Elena laughed softly. 'So what is Rogan supposed to do, hmm? Tie me up and carry me off against my will?'

Blake Rogan made a sound that might have been a laugh. 'I think I'll say goodnight to you now, Señor

Esteban,' he said, and then he turned to Elena. 'Good night, Miss Kelly-Esteban,' he said. 'You'll forgive me if I don't call you *señorita* any more. Now that I've heard your rather fluent English vocabulary, the whole idea of you as some helpless Spanish flower begins to pale.'

Elena's eyes narrowed. 'I don't care what you call me, Mr Rogan,' she said coldly. 'Just make absolutely certain I never have to set eyes on you again.'

Rogan paused beside the patio doors. 'Hold that thought, lady,' he said coldly. 'Frankly, I think it's one hell of a terrific idea.'

He stepped into the house and the door slammed shut behind him.

CHAPTER THREE

ELENA murmured in her sleep and turned her face into the pillow, twisting the sheets and light blanket around her body. In her dream, she was back in the marketplace, hurrying up the hillside that curved above the town square. There were footsteps behind her and the cruel sound of laughter, and now she could feel the hot, rank breath of her pursuers on her neck.

'No,' she whispered, burrowing her face more deeply into the pillow, 'no, don't...'

'Elena...'

Someone was calling her name. In the dream, she gasped for air, drawing it deep into her aching lungs as she raced towards a dark alleyway ahead.

'Elena...'

A man stepped out into the alleyway ahead of her. Yes, she thought, as a fierce exaltation swept through her, yes, it was he. She'd have known those wide shoulders and aggressive stance anywhere. And his eyes, the colour of the midday sky...

'Rogan,' she whispered, 'thank God it's you.'

'Elena!'

She fell against him as she reached him, burrowing into his warm, hard body. His arm slipped around her, and his strength and power seemed to flow into her.

'Rogan,' she said again, 'Rogan...'

'Elena. Elena, you must wake up. *Querida,* please...'

Her eyes flew open suddenly and she stared into her father's face. The bedclothes were tangled around her in a damp knot.

'What is it, Papa?' she whispered. 'What's wrong?'

Her father smiled at her the way he used to when she was little and she'd awaken with a nightmare. He was seated on the edge of her bed, fully dressed as if he were ready to go out for the day. But her bedroom was still in darkness, except for a wavering pool of light that fell over the bed. Candlelight, she thought in surprise, and then she grasped the twisted blanket and sat up. Thunder rumbled in the distance.

'I'm sorry to wake you, Elena,' her father said softly.

She nodded. 'That's all right,' she murmured, running her fingers through her tangled hair. 'Has the power gone off?'

'Elena, you must get dressed.'

She leaned back against the pillows and stared at him. 'I don't understand, Papa. Is something the matter? Are you ill?'

He shook his head. 'No, no, I'm fine. But you must get dressed. There is time to pack a small suitcase, if you wish.' He rose from the bed and she watched as he marched across the room and pulled open her cupboard door. He was all dark shadows now, and his voice was muffled as he leaned into the wardrobe. 'This one will do,' he said, pulling her overnight bag from the shelf and tossing it on the foot of the bed. 'Be quick, Elena. There's not much time.'

Fear roughened her voice. 'Papa, what are you talking about? What's going on?'

'The city is falling,' he said with an abruptness that made the breath catch in her throat. 'Get dressed quickly and come down to the library. There's no time to waste.'

She watched in disbelief as the bedroom door closed after him. What was he talking about? He'd looked so worn lately; perhaps the tensions of the country were too much for him. Elena's heart pounded as she scrambled from the bed and pulled on her robe. She would go downstairs and phone for a doctor. What her father had said—that the city was falling—was insane. Things were bad in San Felipe, yes, but surely not that bad? Her birthday party had only ended a few hours ago, amid laughter and toasts for her health and happiness, even though she'd had to force herself to smile and say all the right things. She had not been enjoying the party to begin with, and Blake Rogan had put the finish to her evening.

If there were fighting in Santa Rosa, she would have heard something wouldn't she? The ranch wasn't very far from town. Well, there was the distant sound of thunder, yes, but that was because of the rain.

The thunder rumbled again and she stirred uneasily. There was a strange, flat quality to the sound, as if someone were setting off fireworks.

'Oh, God,' she whispered as a flash glowed on the horizon. She wasn't listening to the sound of thunder. It was gunfire.

The realisation thrust her into action. Elena hurried to the dresser and began to pull clothing from its drawers. Underthings, shirts, sweaters, whatever her hands fell on was tossed, helter-skelter, into the suitcase and then she snapped it shut.

She stripped off her robe and nightgown. Dress quickly, her father had said, and she did, tugging on the first things she thought of, a pair of jeans and a shirt. Normally, she never wore anything like that in his presence. Such clothing was unfeminine, he said, and belonged in America, not in San Felipe. But she doubted that he would mind how she looked tonight. She pulled on a pair of cotton socks and her sneakers, snatched up the suitcase, and hurried down the stairs.

Her father was waiting in the library. He'd lit her mother's ornate silver candelabra. As she entered the room, he turned to her and held out a brandy snifter.

'Tell me,' she began, and he shook his head.

'Drink this first,' he said.

'No, I don't want it. I...'

'Drink it, Elena.'

Wordlessly, she took the glass from him and sipped at it. The dark, fiery liquid brought tears to her eyes, and she shook her head and handed it back to him.

'I don't like it,' she said.

Her father sighed. 'Do you remember when you were a little girl, *querida*? Your mother and I would sometimes tell you to do something, that it would be for your own good, and you would say, "I don't like it". But we would insist, and eventually you would obey.'

Elena stared at her father. 'You're going to send me away, aren't you?' she said softly.

He reached out and touched his hand to her cheek. There was a tremor in his fingers, and somehow that frightened her more than anything else that had happened so far.

'Elena,' he said softly, 'there is very little time. I just want to tell you that I love you.'

'Then, let me stay with you, Papa. I...'

'And your mother loves you, too, as she watches you from Heaven. She, too, would say that you must do what I tell you. Do you understand, Elena?'

A succession of sharp sounds echoed through the night, closer than they had been before.

'That's gunfire, isn't it?'

Her father nodded. 'We must go now, Elena.'

So, she thought, the trouble was finally upon them. She was surprised at how calm she suddenly felt. Her mother had always told her that the only way to deal with the devil was to face him without fear. Whatever waited outside the house could be dealt with. The anticipation of fear was always worse than the reality.

'Well, then,' she said calmly, 'I suppose we'd better get going. Where are the servants?'

Eduardo Esteban shrugged. 'Gone. I think they knew before it all started. We are alone, child. Give me your suitcase. I've brought the car around front.'

'No, that's OK, Papa, I can carry it. Where are your things?'

But her father was hurrying to the door, impatiently motioning for her to follow him into the dark night.

She settled beside him in the front seat of the Cadillac as he gunned the engine to life. Strange, she thought, staring into the darkness, but she'd never sat in the front seat of this car before. She'd tried, but Juan wouldn't permit it.

'It is not proper, *señorita*,' he'd said, and his dark eyes told her she'd insulted his sense of propriety with her casual American ways.

Come to think of it, she'd never seen her father drive the car, either. It was a night of 'firsts', she thought, and suddenly she had an insane desire to laugh aloud. The sound of guns in the dark, dressing this way in front of her very proper, very old-world father, and now the way they were riding in the Cadillac—but then, she'd never been in the midst of an insurrection before, had she? She took a deep breath.

'Where are we going, Papa?'

He reached across the seat and patted her knee. 'I know what's best for you, *querida*.'

'That's what you told me the first time you sent me off to boarding-school, remember? I was only thirteen, and I begged you not to sent me away. ''I know what's best for you," you said. It was hard for me to understand.'

There was a heavy silence and then her father sighed. 'This time it may be even more difficult for you, Elena.'

The soft hairs on the nape of her neck stirred. 'Meaning?'

'Meaning you must do as I tell you, no matter how distasteful it seems.'

His words held a warning, but of what? Suddenly she thought of the single suitcase. 'Where are we going, Papa?' she asked, trying to control the rising note of concern in her voice. 'You still haven't told me.'

'I'm taking you to safety, child.'

'Are we going north? Are the roads safe?'

'No, I'm sure they're not. But that doesn't matter. Soon, you'll be on a plane headed for Miami.'

'You mean, *we'll* be on a plane...'

'No, Elena. I am staying here, where I belong. You are leaving without me.'

Elena shook her head. 'No,' she said quickly. 'That's out of the question, Papa.'

Her father's voice was sharp. 'You will do as I tell you,' he said. The Cadillac lurched as it whipped around a sharp curve in the road. 'You went to school in the United States, Elena. Your mother was an American. You, yourself, live as an American lives...'

'Don't be foolish, Papa. I'm your daughter. I'm as much a San Felipian as you are. It says so on my passport.'

Eduardo Esteban turned towards her. 'Yes, it does,' he said bitterly. 'And only because of my own foolish pride. Your mother wanted you to have an American passport, but I insisted. You were my daughter, I said, with the blood of the Estebans in your veins. And now...'

Silence filled the car and finally Elena touched her father's arm. 'And now?' she prompted.

'And now I shall remedy that,' he said grimly, pulling the car to the kerb.

A large building stood back from the road, silhouetted against the dark sky. Lights gleamed in several of its windows.

'The American Embassy? Why have we come here?'

Her father was already out of the car. 'Hurry,' he said as he opened her door. 'There's no time to waste.'

Elena scrambled out of the door. 'But they won't let us in,' she said. 'Not in the middle of the night. Not . . .'

Her father gave his name at the gate and the soldiers waved them through. The Embassy compound was a mass of confusion. People were hurrying back and forth in the dark. Elena's father clutched her wrist and pulled her along beside him towards the building entrance.

Was he going to request sanctuary? No, she thought, that couldn't be it. He'd said he was going to put her on a plane headed north. Not that she'd let that happen, she told herself with conviction. Her father could argue all he liked, he could remind her of what an obedient child she'd been, but there was no way she was leaving here without him. *That* was definite.

They were on the second floor of the building now, hurrying down a poorly lit corridor. Her father had said he was going to remedy the fact that she didn't have an American passport, but that was impossible. Nobody in this place was about to issue passports now. You needed all sorts of papers, none of which she had with her. And, even if she had, not even American efficiency would include stopping everything for as long as it took to document those papers and make up a passport in the middle of a revolution.

'Señor Esteban! It's a damned good thing you got here. I wasn't going to wait much longer.' A man had stepped into the corridor from one of the offices. He gestured to them impatiently. 'Come on, come on, let's go.'

Now, suddenly, the taste of fear filled Elena's mouth. She turned to her father, her green eyes searching his face, until finally he looked away from her.

'Papa?'

Her father sighed. 'One moment,' he said to the man, and then he put his arm around Elena's shoulders and began walking her slowly towards the end of the hall. '*Querida,* this is going to be difficult for both of us. Remember, as I talk to you, that I love you and that this will be for the best.'

What was he going to say? Why was he making all these apologies? He was sending her away again, yes, but there was more to it than that. There was something he wanted to tell her, something he was afraid to say...

'What is it?' she pleaded. 'Why are we here?'

'Come on, Esteban, get it over with.'

Elena gasped and spun towards the all too familiar sound of Blake Rogan's voice. He was standing in the doorway of one of the offices, his hands in the pockets of his trousers, watching her through narrowed eyes.

'This conversation doesn't concern you, Mr Rogan,' she snapped. 'My father and I would like some privacy, if you don't mind.'

Rogan laughed. 'Shall I tell her why she's here, Esteban? Or are you afraid she'll be less than thrilled if she hears it from me?'

The light here was better than it had been on the patio a few hours before. She could see Rogan clearly, see every flawlessly tailored inch of his grey suit, his highly polished shoes, even smell the faint scent of what was surely an expensive cologne. But none of it mattered. The man still looked like a bandit, come down from the hills to wreak havoc in the lives of normal people. Elena took a deep breath. It was inconceivable that this man and her father should have discussed her, but clearly they had. She thought back to the curious conversation Rogan and her father had had on the patio, thought of the plans her father had made to fly her home, and a bitter smile touched her mouth.

'Mr Rogan has been hired to get me to the airport,' she said softly. 'Is that right?'

Her father pursed his lips. 'Something like that,' he said.

Rogan laughed again, and the sound made her blood run cold.

'Is there more to it? Has he been hired to escort me all the way to Miami? Is that it, Papa? Well, it doesn't matter. I don't care if he sits on me; I'm not getting on that plane and I'm not...' She broke off in surprise as Rogan moved out of the doorway. He was beside her before she could take a breath, his hand closing tightly around her wrist. 'What the hell do you think you're doing, Rogan? Let go of me. Papa, tell this man to...'

'I thought you said she was a sweet-tempered girl with a docile disposition, Esteban.' Rogan's fingers bit into the tender flesh inside her wrist. 'Go on, tell her.'

'Señor Rogan, please, if you would just give us another minute...'

'You've taken too damn much time as it is,' Rogan growled. As if to underscore what he'd said, there was the thunderclap and an explosion flashed brightly outside the window. 'Tell her, or I will.'

The fear building within Elena was making it almost impossible for her to breathe. She turned to her father and put her hand lightly on his arm.

'Tell me what?' she whispered. 'Please, what is he talking about?'

Her father sighed. 'There is a plane scheduled to leave here soon, *querida*. I have been assured it will do so. I...'

The man who had greeted them minutes earlier put his head into the corridor again.

'Jeez, are you still talking? Dammit man, if you're not ready to go with this in five minutes, I'm leaving. Do you understand?'

Eduardo Esteban nodded and then he turned towards his daughter. 'Listen to me, Elena,' he said, and there was a rough urgency in his voice. 'A plane is leaving soon. There is a place for you on it.'

'Not without you. I...'

For the first time in her life, Elena heard her father curse. He grasped her shoulders and shook her.

'Do not interrupt me again, Elena. You will be on that plane. Do you understand? I will not tolerate any insolence.'

Elena's eyes filled with tears. 'But what will happen to you, Papa? I...'

Esteban smiled tenderly. 'I shall be fine, *querida*, especially if I know you are safe.'

Rogan took a step towards them. 'Will you please cut the crap and get to it, Esteban? That plane's not going to wait for us, you know.'

'Elena, *querida*, listen to me. It is possible—it is probable—that those who carry San Felipian passports will not be permitted to leave the country. Do you see? If you had an American passport, as you should have, you would be able to board the plane.'

Elena shook her head. 'But I don't have one. And I can't believe that the Embassy would be willing to verify my right to one now.'

Her father nodded in agreement. 'Exactly. But if the situation were different—if, for example, you were *married* to an American citizen...'

'But I'm not,' Elena said impatiently.

Esteban stroked the hair back from her forehead. 'But if you were,' he said softly, 'no one could stop you from boarding that plane.'

'Papa, what...'

Rogan's hand closed over her wrist again. 'Which brings us to why you're here.' Elena looked at him blankly and he laughed. 'A quick temper and a short memory. You're no bargain, are you, *señorita*?'

'Señor Rogan, there is no need to be unkind. My daughter...'

Rogan nodded. 'OK,' he growled, looking into Elena's eyes, 'I'll refresh your memory. A few minutes ago, you wanted to know why you were here. Well, it's time someone told you.'

She waited for him to say something else, but suddenly Blake Rogan looked uncomfortable. A fist seemed to clench deep inside her. 'Papa,' she said softly, her eyes still locked with Rogan's, 'what is he talking about?'

Eduardo Esteban let out his breath. '*Querida,* forgive me.' Her father took her hand and placed it in Rogan's. 'You are to be married to this man. When you leave here tonight, it will be as Mrs Blake Rogan.'

CHAPTER FOUR

ELENA snatched her hand from Rogan's and stared at her father in disbelief.

'What did you say?'

'Elena,' he said softly, 'Mr Rogan and I have reached an agreement.'

Had everyone gone crazy? It was the middle of the night, the country was in the midst of an armed insurrection, and her father was making a joke. But his face told her it was no joke. His expression was grim.

'You can just forget all about your agreement, Papa. It's impossible.'

'Listen to me, Elena. Mr Rogan is going to marry you. Then you will be able to leave Santa Rosa in safety. You...'

Her father was still talking, but she'd stopped listening. She looked at Blake Rogan. He was leaning against the wall, arms folded across his chest, watching her in stony silence. An agreement, she thought, as shock gave way to disbelief, disbelief to anger, and suddenly the anger became rage.

'You want me to...to marry this man?' she demanded, cutting into her father's explanation. 'You want me to marry this...this...'

Rogan made a sound that was not quite a laugh. 'Believe me, lady, words fail me, too.'

Her green eyes raked him with cold dismissal before she turned her back to him.

'Is that what you want, Papa?'

Esteban sighed. '*Querida,* you must understand. It is the only way to ensure your safe departure.'

Elena tossed her head and her dark hair swung away from her face. 'I'd rather die,' she said clearly.

This time, Rogan laughed aloud. 'At least we agree on something,' he said, his teeth bared in a feral grin. 'I'm as thrilled with the idea as you are.'

Elena ignored him. 'None of this makes sense, Papa. I won't leave you.'

'You will do as I tell you, Elena,' her father said sharply.

'But if you want me to take that flight, why...'

Rogan cursed softly. 'Come on, Esteban. It's now or never. Tell the princess the details. Time's running out. You do it, or I will.'

Her father's face darkened. 'No,' he said quickly, 'no, I'll talk to my daughter.'

The American grinned. 'Yeah, I thought you'd prefer it that way.' He put his hand in the small of Elena's back and she pulled away from him.

'Don't you touch me,' she said softly. 'Not ever.'

His eyes narrowed. 'Don't make threats, Princess. Not unless you're prepared to back them up.'

'And don't call me that, Mr Rogan. I...'

His hand landed in the small of her back again and she stumbled forward.

'Go on, Esteban. Explain the facts of life to her. And make it snappy. In ten minutes, I leave with or without her.'

Esteban's eyes flashed darkly. 'We have made a deal, Rogan.'

Rogan's eyes narrowed. 'Right—and it's one I could hardly say no to, could I? OK, Esteban. Ten minutes—and if she's not convinced by then, I'll put a piece of tape across her mouth and you can wag her head up and down and make her vows for her.'

Elena's mouth dropped open. 'How can you let him talk to you that way, Papa? How...'

Her father grasped her arm and hurried her to the end of the corridor. 'Listen to me, Elena. Rogan and I have made a deal. He...'

'Have you lost your mind?' she sputtered. 'The man's an animal! He...'

She gasped as her father grasped her shoulders and shook her. 'He's the only way I can be sure of getting you away from here, Elena. For God's sake, think! You carry a San Felipian passport.'

'So what? I...'

'What do you think would happen if they saw the name of Elena Esteban on a passport? Elena Esteban, the daughter of Eduardo Esteban, a government official.'

Elena paled. 'A trusted government official, Papa. All the parties agreed...'

Her father smiled gently. 'Which means I am a valuable piece in the game that will be played in San Felipe over the next months. And a safe one—but not if you remain, *querida*. Not if someone should see my daughter as a means by which I might be controlled.' His hands grasped her shoulders and he stared into her eyes. 'Do you understand, Elena? There would be no way to guarantee your safety—or mine.'

'Papa...'

'Do you understand?' he demanded, his hands grasping her shoulders.

Elena nodded reluctantly. 'Yes,' she whispered, 'I guess I do. But...'

Rogan's harsh voice echoed down the corridor. 'Speed it up, Esteban. You're running out of time.'

'The marriage is only a legal manoeuvre, child. It will give you the name and the papers to get on that plane. When you reach Miami, you and Rogan will go your separate ways. My lawyers will dissolve the marriage as soon as it is legally possible.'

'And...and Rogan agreed to this?' Her father said nothing and Elena moved closer to him. 'I want an answer,' she said stubbornly. 'Why would he go along with this insanity? It can't be out of the goodness of his heart. I know what sort of man he is—he'd have to be blackmailed or bullied into agreeing to something like this.'

'Elena, time grows short.'

'Or he'd have to be bought...'

The man from the Embassy stepped into the hallway again. 'Esteban—it's now or never. I agreed to help you, not to put my neck in a noose.'

'I did what had to be done, Elena. I...'

'You mean you bought him,' she said flatly. 'What did it cost, Papa?'

Her father's eyes darkened. 'A great deal,' he said softly, and a strange expression slid across his face. But then he shook his head and smiled at her. 'And it was worth it.'

Elena's eyes glittered with unshed tears. 'Papa,' she whispered, 'please—don't ask me to do this.'

'It is for the best, Elena.'

There was nothing left to say after that, and she hung her head in silent acquiescence. After that, everything seemed to happen all at once. Her father hurried her into the lighted office, and then Rogan was standing beside her and the man from the Embassy was mumbling words that she had sometimes dreamed of hearing, but not like this, not while she stood in a room filled with metal filing cabinets and typewriters, with the sound of gunfire in the streets and a stranger at her side.

The Embassy man paused and stared at Blake Rogan.

'Come on, man,' he muttered. 'Say it.'

Rogan cleared his throat. 'I do,' he mumbled, staring straight ahead of him.

And then it was her turn. But she couldn't. She couldn't...

'Speak the words, Elena,' her father whispered, but her tongue felt as if it were fastened to the roof of her mouth.

'Say it,' Rogan muttered. His hand sought hers and his fingers squeezed her wrist until she drew in her breath. 'Come on,' he said impatiently, 'finish it.'

'I do,' she gasped, and it was all over. Blake Rogan was her husband.

An automatic smile appeared on the Embassy official's face. 'Well,' he said, extending his hand towards Rogan, 'congrat...' Their eyes met and the official's face reddened. 'OK,' he said, clearing his throat. 'That's that. I've—er—I've got some papers for you here, Mrs...uh, *señorita*. I—er—I wish you well...'

Elena nodded stiffly. 'Thank you.'

The man gave her a quick smile. 'No problem. And now I think we'd all better get the hell out of here.'

A series of distant explosions rattled the windows, underscoring his words.

Rogan took Elena's arm. 'OK,' he snapped, 'let's move it.'

Elena turned towards her father, tears streaming down her cheeks. 'Papa...'

But Rogan was already moving her forward, his arm around her waist, the fingers splaying across her hip.

'Come on, lady. Give Daddy a kiss and let's go.'

'Damn you, Rogan,' she cried, 'don't you tell me what to do! I'm not taking orders from...'

The breath caught in her throat as he hauled her towards him. 'You'll take orders and like it, Princess. I'm in charge here—and don't you forget it for a minute. Until that plane lands in Miami, you'll do exactly as you're told.'

Elena's eyes glittered with tears of rage. 'My father won't let you...'

A quick, feral grin lit Rogan's face. 'Won't he?'

Elena looked at her father and his mouth twisted. 'She is my daughter, Rogan,' he said softly. 'Remember that.'

Another explosion sounded outside, closer than the last, and this time the floor trembled under their feet.

'Let's go, people.'

Esteban put his arms around Elena. *'Vaya con Dios, querida,'* he whispered, kissing her on the cheek. 'Go with God.'

She wanted to tell him that the man he was sending her with was further from God than anyone she'd ever met in her life, but Rogan's hand was around her wrist and he was tugging her out of the door after him. Her feet almost flew out from under her as they rounded a corner into a dimly lit corridor.

'Pay attention to what you're doing,' he snapped.

'My father,' she whispered, and then her throat closed with emotion. It was just as well, she thought as Rogan pushed open a fire door. He'd never be able to understand what she was feeling. A man like that probably felt no human emotions. Ahead of them, a flight of stairs plunged downwards.

'Come on, come on. Move it.'

He tugged at her hand as they clattered down the steps, her feet flying faster than she thought possible. Rogan's fingers were a steel clamp around her wrist; she could feel her hand going numb beneath their pressure. She'd been right about him from the beginning. He was an adventurer, all right, and never mind the expensive suit and the fancy cologne. He was worse than an adventurer—he was a man who would do anything if the price were right, a man who would even sell his name.

The lights in the stairwell flickered and died as they reached the bottom step. Elena stumbled in the sudden darkness and Rogan's arm slid around her.

'Easy,' he said softly, holding her in the curve of his arm. He moved ahead slowly, stopped and lit a match. 'OK,' he whispered, 'let's go. There's an exit door at the end of the corridor. Can you see it?'

Elena nodded. 'Yes.'

Rogan blew out the match and they groped their way to the door.

'We'll leave from the rear of the building. There's a stretch of grass and then a stone wall. When we get outside, I want you to run like hell for that wall and get over it, fast. Understand?'

She nodded again. 'Yes.'

'Don't stop for anything. Never mind what you see or hear. Just get over that wall.'

Her skin prickled with uneasiness and she turned towards him, sensing his nearness in the darkness.

'What about you?' she whispered. 'Won't you be with me?'

'I'll be right beside you, Princess,' he said, and she heard the laughter in his voice. 'You don't think I'd get too far from my bride on our wedding night, do you?'

Anger and humiliation coursed through her as he pushed past her and opened the door.

'God, how I hate you,' she whispered. 'I . . .'

She gasped as he slapped her lightly on the bottom. 'Save the tender words for later,' he murmured. 'Now, go on. Run!'

He gave her a quick shove and suddenly she was outside the building, running across the grounds in the darkness. The wall was ahead of her, just as he'd said it would be, a stretch of blackness against the charcoal sky. She could hear the sound of their footfalls, but everything else was silent. The compound—at least, what she could see of it—was deserted.

The wall loomed ahead, higher and broader than it had seemed from a distance. Elena's footsteps slowed.

'Keep going,' Rogan whispered.

'Isn't there a gate?' she panted. 'I can't . . .'

'Yes, you can,' he said, grasping her hand in his. 'You have to.'

'I can't. I . . .'

Rogan caught her around the hips and lifted her up to the wall. 'Go on, grab hold. That's it,' he said as her fingers scrambled for purchase on the rough stone surface, 'that's the way. Hurry!'

She dug her fingers in as he shoved her unceremoniously from below until finally she was perched on top of the wall. A grunt and some scrambling, and Rogan was beside her. He dropped quickly to the ground on the other side and held his arms up to her.

'Jump.' Elena hesitated and he shifted impatiently. 'I won't drop you, for God's sake.'

No, she thought, looking down at him, he wouldn't. And it wasn't really much of a jump. Then what was holding her back? She looked at him again, at his outstretched arms waiting to enclose her, and then she took a deep breath and let herself go.

Rogan caught her to him and set her down. 'OK. My car's parked just over there. Do you see it?'

'Yes. I ... Wait a minute,' she said quickly.

'What's the matter now?'

'I have a suitcase—I left it in my father's car.'

His arm encircled her. 'You don't need it.'

'But ...'

'Listen, Princess, if you follow orders and behave yourself, you'll be in Miami in a couple of hours. You can buy yourself new make-up and clothes when you get there, OK?'

She thought of the framed photos of her parents that she'd tossed into the valise at the last moment, and a bitter smile touched her lips.

'Sure,' she said. 'No problem.'

She got into the car and stared into the darkness while he shoved the key into the ignition. Good, she thought. Rogan wanted to be rid of her as much as she wanted to be rid of him. That certainly simplified things. There would be no fumbling attempts at conversation during the flight to Miami. Once they were on the plane, they didn't even have to sit together. All they had to do was get past passport control and then they never had to look at each other again. Her father would ... Pain knifed through her as she thought of her father. *Papa* ...

Rogan's harsh voice breached the silence. 'How well do you know these roads?'

Elena blinked. 'What?'

'The roads. Do you know them well? You were brought up here, weren't you?'

She shook her head. 'I ... I don't know,' she whispered.

'You don't know? What kind of an answer is that?'

'I was ... I was thinking about my father ...'

'I didn't ask you about your father,' he said impatiently. 'I asked you about the damned road. Is there another way to get to the airport besides this?' He glanced at her and then back at the road. 'Is there a short-cut?'

She looked at him blankly. 'I'm not sure. I...'

The car skidded from side to side as Rogan stepped on the brakes. Elena fell forward as they came to a sudden stop, and then he reached across the seat and grabbed hold of her.

'I'm only going to say this once, Princess, so you'd damned well better pay attention,' he said, putting his hand beneath her chin and roughly lifting her face to his. 'Are you listening?'

In the darkness, she could see little of his face, but anger gleamed brightly in his eyes. Elena nodded.

'You're worried about your father. Is that right?'

'Of course I am. I...'

'Uh huh. You're concerned about his safety.'

Slowly, she nodded again. 'Yes.'

Rogan smiled. 'That's touching,' he said softly, and then, without warning, he took her by the shoulders and shook her. 'But it doesn't help us one damned bit,' he snarled. 'I'm telling you right now, *señorita*, you'd better stop worrying about your old man's neck and start worrying about your own. Do you understand?'

Elena swallowed. 'Yes,' she whispered. 'The soldiers. And the rebels. But...'

Rogan laughed unpleasantly. 'I'm the one you have to worry about, lady. Not the rebels. Not the soldiers. Just plain old me!'

She twisted against his hands. 'You're hurting me, Rogan...'

'You're nothing but excess baggage, Princess. Spoiled excess baggage, at that. If I were on my own, I'd be half-way to Mexico by now. Instead, I'm sitting in the middle of a road in the middle of the damned jungle...'

The sorrow that had almost overwhelmed her began to recede as her anger grew. The man was making it sound as if he were doing all this as a humanitarian gesture! Elena's shoulders stiffened.

'Aren't you leaving something out of this, Rogan? You'd be half-way to Mexico and a hell of a lot poorer.'

His brows drew together. 'What are you talking about?'

She swivelled away from him. 'I don't know how much my father had to pay you before you'd agree to marry me . . .'

He laughed softly as he started the car again and pulled on to the road. 'You mean Daddy didn't tell you the price of your freedom, Elena?'

Heat flooded her cheeks. 'No,' she snapped. 'He didn't. But he made it clear that it cost a great deal. So don't try to sound like a martyr, Rogan. You're being well paid for what you're doing. Besides, your part in this is just about over. You married me and now all you've got to do is get us to the airport . . .'

' . . . and on that plane. Yeah, it sounds easy enough. But it may not be. We haven't run into any trouble so far, but who knows what might happen between now and flight time? All I'm telling you is that you'd better behave yourself and follow orders until we're out of here. Is that clear?'

'Believe me, Rogan, I . . .'

'Jesus!'

He jammed his foot down on the brake pedal and the car slewed across the road. Elena braced her hand against the dashboard as they came to a sliding stop.

'It's a roadblock,' she whispered.

Rogan laughed sharply. 'No kidding.'

She stared out of the windscreen at a pair of vehicles angled across the narrow road. The glare of Rogan's headlights picked out the shapes of three men moving slowly towards them, rifles clasped in their arms.

'Rogan? Do you think they're soldiers?'

He shook his head. 'They're not wearing uniforms.'

A tremor danced along Elena's spine. 'Then they're not police, either. That means they must be rebels...'

'Or bandits. When a country starts to sink, the scum always surfaces.' The three men were almost at the car. One of them switched on a flashlight and directed the beam into their eyes. 'Listen,' Rogan said quietly, 'you just keep quiet and let me do the talking, OK?'

'Yes, but...'

'No "buts", Elena,' he said harshly. 'All you've got to do is keep your mouth shut. Can you manage that?'

She nodded. 'Yes, all right. I just hope you know what you're doing, Rogan. I...'

'We're on our honeymoon,' he muttered. 'Just remember that... *Buenas noches,*' he said as he rolled down his window. *'Buenas noches, compadres.'*

His voice was pleasant and smooth. But his Spanish, so perfect in the market-place two weeks before, was unmusical and clumsy. Elena looked at Rogan in surprise. He was babbling away in a combination of broken Spanish and English, talking a blue streak at the three men who were standing beside the car.

'...never dreamed the little lady and I would find ourselves in the middle of so much excitement,' he said, putting his hand over hers. 'Say hello to the gentlemen, sweetheart.'

Elena forced a smile to her lips. 'Hello,' she said, staring at the men. There was a sullen unpleasantness to their faces. The one with the flashlight pointed it into the back seat and then motioned to them.

'I think he wants us to step outside, sweetheart,' Rogan said, clasping her hand in his. 'Let's just oblige them.'

Rogan's arm came around her as they got out of the car. Elena shivered, uncertain as to whether it was from the sudden dampness of the night air or from fright.

'Rogan?' she whispered.

He drew her more closely against him. 'It's all right, love,' he said. She knew, by the way he spoke, that he wanted the men to hear him. 'Just think of what an exciting story we'll have to tell when we get back to the States.'

She shivered again as she burrowed against him, and his arm tightened around her, the hard warmth of his body offering her comfort. The men poked into the car's interior, mumbling softly to each other. One of them turned to Rogan and snapped his fingers.

'What does he want?' Elena murmured.

'He wants his throat slit,' Rogan said pleasantly. 'But I suspect he'll settle for the keys. Here, *compadre*,' he said, tossing them to the man. 'Take a look in the trunk, if you like.'

'Suppose he understands English, Rogan? Suppose...'

'Easy, Princess. You just concentrate on looking like a blushing bride.'

'Yes, but...'

The keys landed at their feet with a metallic jingle. Rogan picked them up and grinned at the three armed men.

'What you doing here?' the smallest—and meanest-looking—demanded.

'I told you,' Rogan said easily. 'We're on our honeymoon.'

The men conferred together and then the small one turned to them again. 'Why here, in San Felipe? There has been—talk, *si*?—talk of trouble here...'

Rogan grinned and drew Elena against him. 'Yeah, I guess. We've been travelling for a couple of weeks, you see, and we were so busy with other things that we just didn't pay too much attention.' He chuckled softly and bent his head to hers. 'You know how it is when you've only been married a little while.'

His lips touched Elena's cheek. The men mumbled among themselves and then they laughed. The small one said something to the others, something crude that Elena understood all too clearly. She drew in her breath, but before she could speak, Rogan's fingers bit into her flesh, warning her to remain silent.

'Well, if you guys don't mind, we're going to move along now,' he said. His hand urged her forward and immediately the three men tensed. 'It's getting kind of late and we want to get some miles on us before morning.' One of the men shifted position and his rifle barrel began to move. 'Lovely country you have here, fellas.'

Elena moved forward slowly, her eyes never leaving the moving rifle. 'Rogan?'

'Keep going, Elena,' he whispered. 'That's the girl. Now, get into the car.'

She did as he told her, an empty smile on her face as she slid across the front seat. Despite the coolness of the night, sweat had plastered her clothing to her body. The men watched in silence and then, suddenly, the tallest of the three stepped forward and angled his rifle towards the car. Elena heard Rogan's swift intake of breath; quickly, before he could respond, she scrambled across the seat and hooked her arm around his neck.

'Ask them if they know of some sweet little inn where we can stay the night, Blake honey,' she said quickly. Rogan's eyes registered sudden understanding and something more. She managed a girlish giggle as she pressed her face into his shoulder. 'I know you wanted to drive straight through to the border, but after all this excitement, I'd really like to, you know, stop for a while.'

There was silence again. Elena kept her face buried against Rogan's jacket, but every fibre of her being concentrated on the sounds outside the car. She could hear the shift of feet on gravel, hear the whispered voices, and then, finally, the raucous sound of male laughter. The smallest of the men called out something and he slapped the car door with his hand.

'*Vamos,*' he said.

Blake stepped down on the accelerator. 'Yeah,' he muttered, 'I agree. Let's get the hell out of here.'

Elena breathed a sigh of relief as the car shot forward. 'Thank God,' she whispered.

Blake glanced at her. 'Don't be so modest, Princess,' he said with a soft laugh. 'That was pretty quick thinking. You got us out of a tough spot.'

'I hoped it would work. Latin men sometimes get so caught up in being male that they forget everything else. I mean, I figured if I could get their minds off other things and on me...'

'Well, it sure as hell worked. You almost had me convinced.'

The car swayed through a curve and Elena suddenly realised she was still sitting tucked tightly against him. A blush spread across her face and she scooted across the seat until she was as far from him as the narrow confines of the car would permit.

'I'm just glad it worked,' she said, staring straight ahead.

Blake laughed. 'The honeymoon's over, hmm? Well, thanks anyway, Princess. For a couple of minutes there, I was afraid I was going to have to take on the three of them.'

'Three men and three rifles?' She shuddered. 'You'd have lost.'

He laughed softly. 'Maybe.'

Her eyebrows rose. 'Maybe? Aren't you over-estimating your abilities, Rogan?'

'Blake,' he said. 'It sounds more convincing if you call me by my first name. After all, I'm your husband, remember?'

'Only for the next ten minutes or so, *Mr* Rogan,' she said with deliberate emphasis. 'The airport is just over that rise. We should be able to see the lights from it any minute now.'

He nodded. 'Maybe we're going to make it, after all. What the hell, except for that little run-in we just had, it's been quiet ever since we left the Embassy.'

Elena turned towards him. 'What do you mean, "maybe we're going to make it"?' she demanded. 'My father said there was a plane. He said...'

Blake sighed. 'I know what he said, Princess. But he's not a magician. When we left the city, the airport was still in government hands. That was a long time ago. By now...'

'Look,' Elena said, leaning forward, 'do you see the sky?' She pointed to a red glow on the horizon. 'The sun's coming up—it's almost dawn.' A smile curved across her face. 'Maybe the fighting will stop when daylight comes. Maybe...'

Blake threw his arm across her as he stepped on the brakes. The car skidded to a halt at the crest of a hill and Elena drew in her breath as she stared at the airport in the valley below.

It wasn't sunrise that was touching the hills with fire. Everything—hangars, planes, and buildings—was consumed in flame.

CHAPTER FIVE

ELENA stared in horror at the scene that lay below the ridge. The airport buildings were fiery masses of twisted metal, angry red flames still shooting into the sky from the gutted structures. Several small planes were burning brightly; a larger one, next to what had been the terminal, was nothing but a charred ruin.

She heard the rasp of Rogan's breath beside her, and then he sighed. 'Well,' he said finally, 'so much for the plane to Miami.'

'But . . . who would do such a thing? It doesn't make sense. No matter who wins in San Felipe, they need the airport.'

He shrugged as he pulled the car on to the road again. 'What's the difference who did it? The airport's gone. That's all that matters.'

'Yes, but . . .'

'There are no "buts". It's finished. Dead. *Muerte. Comprende,* Princess?'

'Shouldn't we go down and see if there's anybody who needs help?'

'No.'

She looked at him. 'No?'

His voice was rough with impatience. 'It's the same in Spanish and in English. No, Elena. We're not going anywhere except out of here.'

'But there might be people hurt down there. They might need us.'

Blake's eyes scanned the burning wreckage. 'Believe me,' he said in a flat voice, 'there's nobody down there who needs us. Not any more.'

Tears glistened in her eyes. 'How could anyone have done that? It's such a waste...'

'Listen, Princess, if you want to discuss the deeper meaning of what's going on in San Felipe some time, I'd be happy to oblige. We can meet in Miami and talk about it over a drink. For now, I just want to get the hell out of here. Take a look in the glove compartment and see if you can find a map.'

Elena shook her head. 'I don't believe you, Rogan. My country is collapsing all around me, and all you can think of is yourself. Can't you understand how I feel? Don't you have any feelings?'

'Yes,' he said grimly. 'I have this strange attachment to my own neck, and I'm determined to hang on to it. Now, see if there's a map in that compartment.'

'See for yourself,' she snapped. 'It's your car and your neck and... are you crazy?' she gasped, grabbing for the dashboard as he slammed on the brakes. 'You'll kill us, Rogan. You...'

He was across the seat before she could finish the sentence, his hands gripping her shoulders so hard that she could feel each finger imprinting itself in her flesh.

'Spare me the holier-than-thou attitude, Princess. If this is "your country", why do you live in the States?'

'How do you know that?'

His lips curved back from his teeth. 'I'm a real romantic,' he said coldly. 'I found out everything I could about my prospective bride.'

'I don't have to explain anything to you, Rogan. I...'

'Then don't preach to me, either. It wasn't my idea to have you for a travelling companion.'

He was holding her so tightly that she wanted to cry out, but somehow she managed to lift her chin and meet his furious stare with a cold one of her own.

'Meaning?'

His blue eyes narrowed. 'Meaning,' he said softly, 'that you'd better remember who's in charge here, Princess. Otherwise...'

Her eyebrows rose. 'Otherwise?' she challenged.

Blake smiled unpleasantly. 'Figure it out for yourself,' he said, thrusting her from him. 'And if you have difficulty coming to a conclusion, just remember that I can make better time alone than if I have to drag you along with me. *Comprende?*'

'You're a despicable human being, Rogan,' Elena whispered. 'If my father only knew...'

The tyres squealed as he gunned the car forward. 'Your father didn't choose me for my personality. He saddled me with you because he knew you'd never make it without me.'

Elena tossed her head. 'Saddled you? Paid you, you mean, and paid you handsomely, I'll bet.'

Rogan's lips drew back from his teeth. 'Yeah,' he said softly, 'the price was right. But it was for a quick wedding and a plane ride.'

Something in his words chilled her. 'What do you mean?' she asked slowly.

He shrugged. 'Just look for a map, will you? The sun will be up soon and this road won't be the safest place in the world.'

A cold fist seemed to have settled just beneath her heart. 'Listen, Rogan,' she said softly. 'If you've got any ideas about leaving me behind...'

Rogan turned towards her, his eyes glinting with cool amusement. 'Would I abandon my sweet bride?'

The laughter in his voice was barely concealed. Elena felt a flush rise to her cheeks.

'You'd just better remember that you won't collect a penny of your money if you get to Miami without me,' she said. 'My father's lawyers...'

'Is that a threat, Princess?'

His voice was soft as silk, but there was an edge of hardness just beneath it. The cold fist within her knotted tighter and Elena's breathing quickened.

'No,' she said quickly, 'not a threat. Just a reminder. If you want to be paid...'

'Good. Because I'd hate to have to tell you it was an empty threat.'

This time, the silken voice was wrapped around steel. Elena clasped her suddenly trembling hands tightly in her lap.

'Stop playing with me, Rogan,' she said softly, her eyes on his impassive profile. 'What are you getting at?'

He shrugged his shoulders. 'My fee for this job's already been taken care of.'

'That's impossible...'

He grinned. 'Bad business, maybe, but not impossible.'

Elena took a deep breath. 'Are you saying my father paid you in advance?'

Rogan shrugged. 'That was the deal,' he said casually, flexing his shoulders.

'But then...then...'

A wolfish grin spread across his face. 'Yes,' he said. 'Exactly.'

No, she thought, staring at him in disbelief, no, it had to be a lie. Her father wouldn't have done anything so foolish... You didn't pay a man like Rogan in advance; even she knew that. But if Rogan had insisted on getting his money up front, what choice would her father have had except to pay it? Besides, who would have dreamed that the plane that was supposed to take her to safety would end up a charred piece of metal, squatting like an obscene travesty of modern sculpture on a deserted runway?

Now what? she thought, lacing her fingers together. There was no plane to Miami, Rogan had his money, and here they were racing along a road that led God only knew where, while civil war raged all around them.

She glanced at the man beside her. His firm jaw was set, jutting forwards as if he were ready to take on the world. In the grey light of the dawning day, she could see dark stubble already showing on his chin. He'd discarded his tie some time during the previous hours, and his shirt was opened half-way down his chest, showing a profusion of flat, dark curls against tanned skin. The civilised exterior had given way to the real Blake Rogan, she thought, the one she'd known was there all along, the one who was hard and violent and uncaring.

There was only one thing to do. Elena cleared her throat.

'All right,' she said finally, 'take me back to Santa Rosa.'

Rogan shook his head. 'Don't be silly.'

'You can keep the money. I'll tell my father to let you...'

'Jesus,' he said, slapping his hand against the steering wheel, 'don't you ever come down from that ivory tower? I wish to God I *could* take you back to Santa Rosa. Believe me, I'd like nothing better.'

'Then do it. We haven't come that far. We could be there in a couple of hours.'

'We could be dead in a couple of hours,' he snarled. 'Wake up, Elena. Your world is gone. There aren't any more fancy houses and finishing schools.'

'Don't lecture me, Rogan,' she said angrily. 'You don't know anything about me. I...'

'I know all I need to know.'

'Look,' she said, 'there's no point in arguing. Just turn the car around and...'

'Dammit, will you listen to me? There is no going back. Not with everything going to hell in a handbasket. The only good thing about this mess is that the car is pointed north.'

'North,' she repeated. 'Towards the border, you mean?'

Rogan nodded. 'Exactly.'

Her eyes met his. He was right, of course. There was no turning back, if not for her own sake, then for her father's. She knew that, just as she knew that she could never cross the endless miles ahead without Rogan's help. He was watching her through narrowed eyes, waiting, waiting...and suddenly she knew what he was waiting for.

It took all the determination she had to ask what had to be asked. When she finally spoke, her voice was subdued and papery.

'And me?' she whispered.

Rogan shrugged his shoulders, but she was sure she saw the gleam of triumph in his eyes. 'What about you?'

It seemed to take enormous effort to form the words. 'Will you...will you take me with you? Or...'

'Or?'

She swung her head towards him, her eyes bright with anger. Was that laughter she heard in his voice? His eyes were fixed on the road ahead, his mouth a straight line, but there was something in the set of his jaw that told her he was enjoying every minute of her humiliation.

'Look,' she said, her voice tightly controlled, 'let's stop playing games, OK? My father made a deal with you. You were supposed to get me on a plane to the States...'

'You're leaving something out, Princess,' he said softly.

'Leaving what out? I...' Rogan looked at her and grinned, and colour rose quickly into Elena's cheeks. 'All right, yes, you were supposed to marry me. You...'

'Supposed to? I *did* marry you, Elena. How could you forget a ceremony that meant so much to both of us?'

The colour in her cheeks darkened. 'OK, Rogan,' she said through her teeth, 'what's the bottom line?'

He sighed and rubbed the back of his neck. 'You're right, Princess, it's time to put all the cards on the table. It's almost dawn,' he said, leaning over the steering wheel and peering at the pewter-coloured sky. 'I don't want to be sitting here like a target once the sun is up.' He turned towards her and his eyes fixed on hers thoughtfully. 'I could leave you here.' His voice was soft, almost a caress, and Elena felt herself paling beneath it. A cool smile twisted his mouth. 'We both know what a bastard I am, don't we?'

She drew in her breath. 'Listen, Rogan...'

'Come on, don't be shy. You've told me what you thought of me. In fact, you've told me several times.'

'Dammit, Rogan, if you're going to dump me out here, do it! Don't toy with me.'

A muscle clenched in his jaw and he looked back at the road. 'I know it's going to come as something of a disappointment,' he said finally, 'but I'm going to take you with me.'

Her relief was as sweet as a cool breeze on a hot summer's day. She nodded her head and let out her breath. 'Thank you,' she whispered.

The sun was rising over the mountains far ahead of them, its golden rays spreading quickly across the grey landscape. Rogan pulled his sunglasses from his pocket and put them on.

'Don't thank me so quickly, Elena. Not until you've heard me out.'

Elena looked at him, but his eyes, hidden behind the mirrored lenses, were closed to her.

'I don't understand...'

'I'll get us out of here—but I'm not sure how I'm going to do it. There'll be all kinds of problems...'

Her eyes followed his as he looked at the fuel gauge. 'We're all right so far,' she said quickly. 'We've got half a tank of petrol left.'

'You mean, we've already used half a tank.'

'It comes to the same thing,' she said impatiently. 'And we haven't seen anyone since we got away from those three men.'

'Not if you don't count a burned out airport, no.'

'You know what I mean, Rogan. We haven't bumped into a car or a wagon or ..'

'Right. Which makes me wary as hell. This is the main road out of Santa Rosa. And we're in the middle of a rebellion. Where in God's name is everybody?'

He was right, she thought, casting a worried glance out of the window. Everything was much too quiet. Not that she wanted to run into any armed men—the encounter during the night had been quite enough. But wouldn't troops or rebels or somebody be all over this road by now?

'I ... I hadn't thought about it,' she admitted slowly.

Rogan's jaw clenched. 'Well, I have, believe me. Things might get interesting any time now.' He paused and then he looked at her, his expression blank. 'Which brings us back to our deal, *señorita*. If you want me to take you with me . . .

If? She sat up straight and stared at him. 'But you said . . .'

His voice cut through hers. 'If you want my help, you'll have to agree to my terms.'

'Your terms? What do you mean, "terms"? You were already paid to get me out of here, Rogan. You . . .'

He sighed. 'How quickly we forget, Elena. I've already met my part of the deal, remember?'

'But . . .'

'There aren't any "buts". It's not my fault the plane burned, is it?'

Elena drew in her breath. 'That's not the point, Rogan. I . . .'

'You're right, it's not.'

She looked at him quickly. She hadn't expected such a quick concession, but he was smiling agreeably. Dear God, why was she suddenly so nervous? And why was he looking at her that way?

'What terms?' she asked hesitantly.

He shrugged his shoulders. 'I figure I'm entitled to something extra.'

'More money? I haven't got any, Rogan, not here . . .'

'I don't want money,' he said roughly. 'I want something else.'

Her pulse began to pound. 'I . . . I don't understand,' she whispered.

He gave her a smile so dazzling that it made her heart turn over. 'Sure you do, Elena,' he said softly. 'You're my wife. My dutiful wife.'

'I'm not,' she said quickly. 'You know I'm not. We . . .'

He laughed. 'I have a piece of paper that says you are, Princess. Mr and Mrs Blake Rogan—that's us.'

Her mouth fell open and then closed again. She curled into the corner of the seat, wedging herself tightly against the door, and looked at him. His eyes were hidden behind the mirrored lenses of his glasses, but she knew how they must look right now, the midnight-blue irises glinting with amusement at her expense. Her gaze drifted across the high cheekbones that gave his face a mysterious cast. His jaw was thrust forward aggressively, and she could see a muscle ticking in his cheek. She looked at his hands, lying lightly on the wheel of the car, and suddenly she remembered the strength of them when they had held her to him.

They were married. Her father had called it a legal manocuvre, but in the end, all that mattered was that she was Rogan's wife. The piece of paper—the licence that was to have ensured her safety also gave him certain rights, certain privileges. Especially here, she thought, especially in San Felipe, where married women had no rights except those that their husbands permitted.

She felt an unbidden rush of excitement sweep through her. He could do almost anything he wanted to her. She belonged to him. He could stop the car right now, along the side of the road, and turn to her and...and...

But he wouldn't. Blake Rogan might be a lot of things, but he wasn't a man who had to force himself on a woman. Her glance drifted to his mouth and lingered there. His lower lip was full and sensual. Everything about him was sensual. He had the darkest, thickest lashes she'd ever seen. And she could still remember the taste of him, and the touch of his hard hands on her. Heat raced through her blood.

Desperation made her speak. 'I've...I've got a boyfriend in Miami, you know. Did my father tell you?'

Rogan looked at her and grinned. 'No,' he said politely, 'actually, we didn't have time for much chit-chat.'

She felt her cheeks burning with colour. 'We're engaged to be married.'

It wasn't really a lie, she thought. Jeremy had proposed to her twice. The fact that she'd turned him down, the fact that she couldn't imagine him as anything but a nice man and a good employer, was nobody's business but hers. But it might work, she thought, watching Rogan's face. The man had a sense of honour. She knew that much. He'd saved her from those men in the marketplace, hadn't he?

He laughed softly. 'Now, how could that be, Princess? You're already married—to me.'

'We're not,' she said again. 'You know that. And...and Jeremy, my fiancé, would be very angry if you...if you and I...'

'Miami's a thousand miles from here,' he said bluntly.

So much for honour, she thought, closing her eyes. 'You can't really mean that you...that you expect me to...to...'

'I not only mean it, Elena, I demand it.' His voice was suddenly cold. 'I expect you to obey me without question.'

Her eyes flew open. 'Obey you?'

He nodded. 'Yes,' he said curtly. 'I know it's an old-fashioned concept, but it's what I want. You'll do exactly as you're told, when you're told, without argument or questions.' He glanced at her and then back at the road. 'In other words,' he said softly, his voice taking on a hint of cool amusement, 'you'll be the ideal wife.'

The ideal... Hysterical laughter rose in her throat and she fought it back. Rogan had been talking about obedience, not...

'Can you manage that, Elena?'

'I...I suppose I can. I...'

'Getting out of San Felipe isn't going to be a picnic. The last thing I need is to spend every minute explaining my actions to you.' He gave her a quick smile. 'Besides, I'm an old-fashioned man—I like sweet and compliant women.'

It was impossible to prevent herself from snorting. 'I'll bet you do.'

He grinned. 'I haven't had a complaint yet, Princess.'

Elena fell back against the seat and sighed. 'All right,' she said finally. 'We'll do it your way.'

Rogan nodded. 'Good. Now, open that glove compartment and see if there's a map in it. I want to be off this damned road by the time the sun is over that peak.' He dug in his shirt pocket and pulled out a flat box of cheroots. 'And see if there's a pack of matches in there, while you're at it.'

'OK.'

'What's that?'

'I said, OK, Rogan, I heard you.'

'Blake,' he said pleasantly. 'Remember? You want to get in the habit of calling me that, Elena. Who knows how many more times we'll have to convince somebody that we're husband and wife?'

'But that's silly. Who'd know the difference?'

'I would.'

'Yes, but that doesn't make sense, Rogan. It just...'

'Elena!'

Her head snapped up at the sharpness in his voice. 'Yes?'

'We're five minutes into our deal and you're reneging already. No questions, no arguments. Wasn't that the agreement?'

'Well, yes, but you can't mean...'

Blake sighed. 'Sweet and obedient, remember?'

'Rogan, this is ridiculous. I agreed to do as you ask when we're in a situation that requires it. I...'

'Why is this so difficult for you, Elena? I thought all *señoritas* were raised to be dutiful wives.'

'I am not your wife, dammit! I...'

Blake shook his head. 'Don't curse, Elena. I don't like it. My wife...'

'I just told you, I'm not your wife.' The brakes squealed as he pulled the car to the shoulder of the road. 'What are you doing, Rogan? I...'

The angry words caught in her throat as he pulled off his sunglasses and turned towards her. There was something in the taut angle of his body, something in the midnight-blue darkness of his eyes that made her panic. She moved quickly, but not quickly enough. Her shoulders jammed against the door as his hands caught her.

'Lesson one,' he said roughly.

'Don't,' she cried.

He pulled her towards him, his fingers curling in the dark mane of her hair.

'I've tried reasoning with you, Elena.'

'Rogan, I didn't mean...'

His eyes bored into hers. 'No,' he said softly, drawing her closer, 'no, you didn't.'

'Rogan, listen to me...'

'If a marriage licence can't convince you, Elena, maybe this will.'

'Don't,' she said desperately. 'You can't. You...'

He smiled in a way that made her heart stop. 'I can,' he whispered. 'And I damned well will.'

His hand clasped the back of her head and brought her to him. Elena twisted against him, trying to free herself, but it was impossible. His mouth swooped down and caught hers in a kiss that took the breath from her.

She whimpered against his lips, and her hands rose between them, but Blake caught her wrists easily and drew her arms harmlessly to the side.

'Don't fight me, Elena.'

'You bastard,' she hissed. 'I'll kill you. I...'

He laughed softly as he drew her tightly against him and then his mouth covered hers again. She closed her eyes against what was happening, against his punishing kiss. It spoke of ownership and of power, just as his body spoke of strength. She was helpless against him, he was telling her, and she knew it...

And then, suddenly, the kiss began to change. Blake shifted in the seat; his hand fell from her wrists and his arm slid around her, bringing her so closely against him that she could feel her breasts flatten against the hard muscles of his chest. His lips moved over hers, seeking, urging, and then she felt the heated brush of his tongue against her mouth. She murmured something against the silken intrusion and then her lips began to open slowly to his. Her hands slid up his arms, up his shoulders, to his neck.

'Say my name, Elena,' he whispered against her lips, the words searing her like the heated breath of the jungle.

'Please,' she begged, and his mouth closed on hers again.

'Will you say it now?' he murmured a lifetime later.

Her eyes fell closed. 'Yes,' she whispered.

His hands moved down her neck, spreading along her shoulders 'Say it.'

She felt the sting of tears beneath her closed eyelids. 'Blake,' she murmured.

He brought her head against his chest. She could hear his heart beating beneath her ear. A shudder went through her; his heart was racing as rapidly as hers.

'And will you do as I tell you?'

She could feel the heat of his hands burning through her cotton shirt, feel the strange, fiery weakness that seemed to have captured her soul. Her mind struggled against his words.

'Answer me, Elena.'

He cupped her head again and raised her face to his. 'I hate you,' she said in a broken whisper. 'I hate you...'

He laughed softly. 'Do you?'

'Yes,' she said. A shudder went through her as his mouth touched her throat.

'Hate me all you like,' he whispered, touching his tongue to her flesh. 'I don't really give a damn. All I want is your word that you'll obey.'

What would he do if she refused him? The thought sent her blood surging.

'Will you let go if I say I will?'

His voice was thick. 'Are you sure that's what you want?'

For an instant, time seemed to stand still. She felt his arms tighten around her and her heart turned over. She could never fight him off, not if he were determined to have her. What would happen if he began to kiss her again, if he began to touch her? Something quickened and began to uncoil deep within her.

She blinked as his hands fell away from her. 'OK,' he said roughly, jamming the sunglasses on his nose again, 'let's get moving. Where's that damned map?'

CHAPTER SIX

ELENA blinked again, like a dreamer surfacing from a deep sleep. She watched as Blake put his hands on the steering wheel and flexed his fingers. He was staring out of the windscreen, as if he could see something beyond the road arrowing towards the distant mountains. Then, almost imperceptibly, he shook his head and reached for the flat box of cheroots he'd left on the dashboard.

'The glove compartment,' he said, tapping one of the dark cigarillos from the box. His voice was husky, and he cleared it before he spoke again. 'Go on, Elena. See if there's a map in there.'

Her own voice was barely a whisper. 'A...yes, a map...'

Her dark hair, the strands cool against her heated skin, swung forward and brushed against her cheeks as she bent towards the dashboard. What in heaven's name had happened just now? There wasn't much question about why Blake had kissed her. It had been a lesson, just as he'd said, a reminder of how vulnerable and dependent upon him she was. At least, that was how it had started. But it had ended as something quite different, and now her mind was busily skittering away from the possibilities like a nervous horse from the edge of a precipice.

The glove-compartment door was jammed, and she had to slam the heel of her hand against it before it fell open and revealed a dark, littered interior. Half a pack of chewing gum, a pair of sunglasses with one lens missing, a comb, a book of matches—which she tossed to Blake—and finally, in the very rear of the com-

81

partment, a bulky, folded piece of paper. Her fingers closed around it and she pulled it out of the compartment.

'I think this might be... Yes,' she said, 'it's a map.'

The map was ripped along most of its fold, but it was usable. Elena opened it and spread it across the dashboard.

Blake clamped a cheroot between his teeth and nodded. 'Terrific. Let me take a look.'

He bent over the crumpled paper, his head close to hers. She could see the fine lines that fanned out from the corners of his eyes, the furrows beside his mouth. His shoulder brushed against her as he leaned closer to the dashboard. His hair, thick and luxuriant, was the colour of chestnuts, except where the early morning sunlight touched it with gold. It would feel soft to the touch, she thought, her glance flickering to where dark tendrils curled lightly over his collar.

Blake jabbed his finger at a thin blue line. 'This is where we are. And that,' he added, pointing to the top of the map, 'that's where we want to go.'

'Mexico?'

He nodded again. 'Mexico. That's the first stop where we can be sure nobody will make trouble for us just for the hell of it.' He sat back and picked up the matches she'd tossed him. 'But,' he said thoughtfully, 'we've got a problem.'

Elena looked from the map to him. 'Yes, I see. There's only the one road north.'

'Right.'

'And you don't think it's safe to stay on it.'

He nodded as he struck a match and touched the flame to the tip of the cheroot. 'Right again,' he said, peering at the map once more. Two vertical creases appeared between his eyebrows, and a thin plume of smoke drifted up from the cheroot. 'But there's a secondary road ahead of us,' he added, pointing to a thready line that angled to the north-east. 'It leads into the mountains.'

Elena nodded. 'Las Montanas de la Luna. The Mountains of the Moon.'

'Yeah. And just the other side of the mountains, we can pick up the highway again. From there, it's a straight run to Mexico.'

She looked at him warily. 'Aren't you forgetting something? There's the border crossing into Mexico after the mountains.'

Blake shrugged. 'Piece of cake.'

'And the mountains are supposed to be full of bandits.'

He blew a plume of smoke upward and grinned at her. 'Maybe.'

'And we'll have to cover a couple of hundred miles without any supplies or provisions or...'

He took the cigarillo from his mouth and examined the glowing tip. 'Have you got any better ideas?'

Elena sighed. 'No,' she said finally. 'Not one.'

'OK,' he said as he folded the map, 'then that's the plan. If the scale on the map is accurate, we should run into the turn-off in another couple of hours, and there's a town called Las Palmas just north of here. We can buy some food and fill the petrol tank.'

Elena nodded. 'I'll draw up a list of things we'll need.'

'Perfume, lipstick, hairspray...'

She swung her head towards him. A rush of angry words were on her tongue, but the expression on his face stopped her. His lips were curved in a smile, but it held none of the mocking amusement she'd anticipated. After a second, she gave him a quick smile of her own in return.

'Quinine tablets, aspirin, insect repellent,' she said. 'Tinned foods, blankets. And a machete.'

His expression was blank. 'A machete,' he repeated.

'That's rough country up there.'

'Well, well, well,' Blake said softly.

Elena looked up quickly, again expecting that cold look of laughter to be in his eyes. That it wasn't there confused her.

'What does that mean?' she demanded.

He shrugged. 'I guess I'm surprised to find that you haven't spent your life pouring tea and attending débutante dances.'

A flush rose to her cheeks. 'You think you know everything about me, don't you? Has it ever occurred to you that you might have jumped to some conclusions that day we met?'

'Maybe.' He started the car and pulled on to the road. 'Of course, I might ask you the same question.'

'I didn't jump to any con...' She broke off as he looked at her. 'All right, perhaps I did. I thought you were...at first, I assumed you were trying to...'

Blake laughed. 'Yeah, I know what you thought. I'm just surprised you didn't trot out your fiancé and dangle him in front of me right then and there.'

'My fiancé?'

'Yeah, your fiancé.' He grinned at her. 'Don't tell me he's that forgettable, Princess.'

Her fiancé, she thought. *Jeremy*... Dear God, she'd almost forgotten the story she'd told Blake only hours before.

'No,' she said quickly, 'of course not. I...I just forgot I'd mentioned him to you, that's all.'

'You did more than mention him, Elena. You held him out like a talisman for protection.'

'Don't be silly. I did no such thing. I simply told you that...'

'You told me he'd be very upset if I put a move on you.' He glanced at the mortified expression on her face and laughed softly. 'Oh yes, Princess, I know what was going through your pretty head. You thought I was going to demand my conjugal rights.'

Elena felt a blush rise upwards from the very tips of her toes. 'No, I didn't. I . . .'

Blake sighed as he shifted his long legs. 'You sure as hell did. And you thought telling me about old Jeremy would turn me off.' He looked at her again and a lazy grin spread over his face. 'Don't try and deny it.'

'I'm not going to dignify that with a response,' she said turning away from him.

He laughed aloud. 'That's as good as an admission, Princess. You thought . . .'

'And that's another thing,' she said quickly. 'I wish you'd stop calling me that.'

He looked at her in surprise. 'Princess? But it suits you. It . . .'

'Why? Because you think I'm a spoiled little rich girl who's used to getting her own way?'

He shrugged his shoulders. 'I didn't say that,' he said mildly.

'But it's what you think, isn't it?'

He shrugged again. 'You're Elena Kelly-Esteban,' he said slowly. 'Your father is a government official in San Felipe. That means you've grown up like a princess in a fairy-tale kingdom, getting what you wanted whenever you wanted it, pampered by Daddy and everybody else.' He glanced at her and then looked back at the road. 'How's that for a thumbnail sketch?'

'Wrong,' she said stiffly.

He smiled. 'What part's wrong, Princess? The name? I know there's probably a whole bunch of Marias and Teresas and Lucindas in there, but . . .'

She opened her mouth and turned towards him, ready to point out that while his assessment of her was wrong, it was also none of his business. But there was a strange look in his blue eyes, a questioning intensity that made her suddenly want to correct his impression of her. All the angry words that had been on the tip of her tongue melted into silence.

'The only part you got right was the name,' she said finally. 'Well, the Teresa, anyway. As for the rest...' Elena sighed and leaned her head back against the seat. 'My father wasn't always an official. He was an archaeologist. He spent most of his time in the Yucatan Peninsula, digging at Mayan ruins.'

'But you didn't, Princess. I mean, I have a hard time picturing you poking through piles of dirt and old bones.'

She smiled and shook her head. 'No, I stayed at home, on the ranch.'

'With Mama.'

'With Pilar. And Ysabel. And Margarita. And...' She glanced at Blake's puzzled face and she began to laugh. 'I stayed at home with an endless succession of housekeepers. My mother was a painter, Blake. She specialised in wildlife studies, so she went with my father. They were very much in love. I don't think they ever spent a day apart from each other.'

Blake's eyebrows rose. 'Your parents spent their time tramping through the jungle while you stayed home alone in that big house?'

'I wasn't alone,' she said quickly. 'I told you, there were housekeepers.'

'Right. Ysabel and Pilar—and Sleepy, Sneezy and Doc. But you were just a kid.'

'They were all very kind. But they didn't spoil me, believe me. Pilar thought *señoritas* should be seen and not heard. Margarita thought I should learn to remember the less fortunate among us by fasting once a week. And Ysabel, who was very devoted to my mother, convinced her that it would only make it more difficult for me if my parents came home for visits more than twice a year. So...'

'Twice a year? That's all you saw them?'

Elena shrugged her shoulders. 'I'm sure they loved me,' she said. 'But they...'

Her words trailed off and Blake cleared his throat. 'And then Daddy became a government official and life improved.'

'And then the coalition government convinced my father to accept a post, and he and my mother came home, yes.' She smiled at the memory. 'It was wonderful. I'd never been so happy.'

Her voice grew wistful and Blake looked at her. '*Then* they spoiled you,' he said in a gently teasing tone.

'They spoiled me to death for six months. And then Mama talked my father into taking us on a trip into the mountains...'

'The ones we're heading for?'

'No,' she said, shaking her head, 'not those. She wanted to do some sketches of a rare bird that nests in the crater of an extinct volcano. Papa didn't want to go, but she talked him into it. So we bought supplies...'

'Which is why you know what we'll need for the Mountains of the Moon?'

She nodded. 'Yes. The terrain's very much the same.' Her voice lapsed into silence and Blake glanced at her.

'And? Did you go to this volcano?'

Elena nodded again. 'Yes,' she said, and she took a deep breath. 'We went. And...and my mother had an accident. Not while we were at the volcano; it was the day we were heading home. We were crossing the street outside the hotel—we'd stayed there the last night because our plane was leaving early the next morning— and there was a car. It was no one's fault. It just...'

Her words drifted away. Blake glanced at her and then his hand closed over hers.

'Hell,' he said roughly, 'I'm sorry, Elena. I'd never have brought it up if I'd known.'

She made a quick little gesture with her shoulders. 'I . . . I don't even know why I told you,' she said softly. 'I don't talk about it much.'

'And that's when Daddy—when your father sent you off to boarding-school.'

Elena nodded. 'Yes. Between his official duties and his grief . . . It was the best thing, I suppose.'

'And you've lived in the States ever since.'

She nodded again. 'Yes. In Miami. It was where I'd gone to school. And my mother's family is there . . .' She drew in a breath and blew it out. 'This is the first time I've really been back in San Felipe in three years,' she said, and she gave a quick, bitter laugh. 'Three years, and I walked into this mess. Can you believe it?'

Blake squeezed her hand. 'You're asking the wrong person, Princess,' he said, flashing her a quick smile. 'I'm the guy who'd always wanted to visit Mauna Loa.'

Elena looked at him. 'The volcano in Hawaii?'

'And finally I did—the day it erupted.'

She sat up straight and eyed him warily, the ghost of a smile on her lips. 'You're making that up.'

He grinned and shook his head. 'I wish I was. So you see, you're not the only one who has lousy timing.'

They both laughed, and then Elena shifted sideways in the seat and looked at him.

'I'll bet you've been in a lot of interesting places.'

'Well, I've been in a lot of places, that's for sure.' He turned towards her and smiled. 'Some of them aren't as great as they're supposed to be.'

'But you like to keep moving,' she said.

Blake shrugged. 'I've never lived any other way.'

There was a strange tightness in her throat. 'Haven't you . . . haven't you ever thought about trying it?'

'Settling down in one place, you mean?' He chuckled softly. 'There's a whole world out there, Princess, and I've only seen part of it. Why would a man turn down a chance to see it all?'

Elena nodded. It was all too easy for her to picture him drifting from country to country, from town to town, never staying in one place long enough to call it home. That was the kind of man he was; she'd known it from the start. But the image brought with it a curious sense of sadness—which was stupid, she told herself, watching Blake's profile as he concentrated on the road ahead. After all, the way he lived his life was none of her business.

The car rounded a curve and suddenly there was a dusty clearing ahead. A handful of straggly palm trees pointed towards the sky.

'We're here,' she said. 'Las Palmas.'

Blake nodded. 'A metropolis,' he said, easing his foot from the accelerator pedal. 'Just look at all those people.'

She chuckled. 'Yes, it's booming.' The only visible citizens of Las Palmas were two old men, seated on a bench outside what seemed to be the only store. 'Still, that's a good sign, isn't it? If there were soldiers or rebels around, those two wouldn't be sitting there.'

'Well, we don't have much choice anyway. We're damned near running on empty. And my guess was right: there's a petrol pump.' Blake pulled up beside it and shut off the engine. 'Here,' he said, pulling some bills from his pocket, 'you go on into the shop and buy us some supplies.'

'I have money. . .'

His blue eyes met hers. 'You're my wife, remember?' He gave her a teasing grin as he put the bills into her hand and folded her fingers over them. 'What's mine is yours, Princess. Now, go on, see what there is to get us.'

Not much, she thought, staring around her at the almost barren shelves of the little store. The place looked as if it had been ransacked. She peered into every corner and searched every shelf, but all she could come up with were two tins of anchovies, three tins of something she couldn't identify because the labels were missing, a couple of dusty bottles of San Miguel beer, and a leaking box of rice.

She turned to the shopkeeper, who had trailed along after her with a nervous smile on his face.

'Are these the only foodstuffs you have for sale, *señor*?' she asked in the soft, up-country Spanish of the area.

He nodded. 'I'm afraid so, *señorita*,' he said, wiping his hands on his dingy apron. 'There was more this morning, but . . .' He shrugged and held out his hands in apology.

Her pulse quickened. 'I'm afraid I don't understand,' she said pleasantly.

The shopkeeper made a mumbled reply about people who had bought out his stock because of fighting in the city.

'I am sorry, *señorita*.'

She looked at his downcast face and nodded. 'I see. Well, then, I'll just take these things,' she said, dumping the armful of items on the counter and counting out enough *quetzals* to pay for them. Her gaze fell on two ancient cans of insect repellent, and she added them to her purchases.

By the time she got outside, Blake had finished filling the tank. 'That's it?' he asked as she put her sack of groceries into the back seat.

Elena climbed into the car beside him and slammed the door. 'I'm afraid so.' The car sprang forward as she told him what the shopkeeper had said.

'Yeah, it figures. That's the first sign that things are falling apart. I'll feel better when we're off this road.'

She let out a gusty sigh. 'Well, if the map's right, the turn-off is just ahead.'

'The sooner the better.' Blake glanced over his shoulder at the paper sack lying on the back seat. 'At least you got us some supplies.'

'Not very many. And none of the important stuff— no quinine, no aspirin, no machete . . .'

He grinned and reached beneath the seat. 'Scratch the machete off your list, Princess,' he said, brandishing one.

'My God,' she whispered. Gingerly, she took the big, broad-bladed knife by its wooden handle and stared at it. 'Where did that come from?'

'Modesty prevents me from telling you that I liberated it from the uninteresting life it was leading, propped against the gas pump.'

'Then don't,' she said, laughing as she lay the machete on the floor beneath her feet.

'I offered to buy it, but those two old codgers who were baking themselves in the sun refused to talk to me. As for quinine and aspirin, I have some in my luggage.'

Elena looked at him in surprise. 'Luggage?'

He nodded. 'Luggage. We were supposed to be on a plane this morning, remember?'

The smile fell from her lips. 'Yes,' she murmured, 'I remember.'

Blake glanced at her. 'We'll be OK, Princess.' She said nothing and he slipped his arm around her. 'You're just worn out,' he said softly. 'You need some rest.' She stiffened as his hand cupped the curve of her cheek, but finally she let him draw her head down to his shoulder. 'Close your eyes for a while, Elena.'

'I'm OK,' she said, 'really. I . . .'

His hand caressed her cheek slowly, and after a moment she did as he'd suggested. Blake's arm tightened around her. She wouldn't sleep, she thought. She couldn't, not at a time like this. But there was a warm comfort in being held so closely against his hard body. Funny, she thought, but just a few hours ago, she'd have crossed the street if she saw him coming. And now . . . and now . . .

'Elena. Elena, come on, wake up.'

She awoke to the squeal of brakes and the harsh urgency of Blake's voice. 'What is it?' she whispered. 'Why have we stopped.'

'There's a roadblock ahead,' he said. 'See it?'

The road dipped ahead of them, a serpentine series of curves gleaming in the afternoon sun. Elena sat up straight and stared out of the windscreen, trying to see whatever Blake had seen. Finally, she shook her head.

'No, I don't. I . . .'

'Look,' he said, touching his hand to her cheek. 'Turn your head. That's it. Look down there.'

'I still don't see . . .' The breath caught in her throat. Far below them, a pair of army trucks angled across the road. As she watched, men in camouflage suits jumped from the backs. Sunlight glinted on the weapons cradled in their arms. 'Dear God,' she whispered, putting her hand lightly on Blake's arm. 'What do we do?'

But he was already moving, shifting into reverse and slamming the car into a squealing turn. 'We go back,' he said grimly.

'Back? We can't go back. We . . .'

'We passed a turn-off while you were sleeping,' he said, stepping down hard on the accelerator. 'Five or six miles back.'

'The one we were looking for? Why didn't you ...'

'No, not the one on the map. This was just a dirt track. A wagon trail, probably.' Blake glanced into the rear-view mirror. 'It was just an excuse for a road—but we haven't got much choice.'

Elena's eyes followed his. 'Is there anyone following us? Did they see us?'

He shook his head. 'No, I don't think so. But I'll feel a hell of a lot better when we get off this highway. There's the turn-off. I think you'd better brace yourself for a rough ride, Princess,' he said as he swung the wheel hard to the right. The car bounced on to a narrow, packed-dirt trail. 'I just wish to hell we had four-wheel drive.'

Heavy foliage closed around them immediately. The narrow road cut through the trees and tall grass like a thin brown ribbon, and the car groaned in protest as Blake urged it forward.

Elena's teeth clattered together as they hit a deep rut. 'You were right,' she said, raising her voice so she could be heard over the clank and squeal of metal. 'It's not much of a road, is it?'

'No, but it's all we've got. Just call out if you see us aimed at something.'

Tall trees crowded in from each side, and thick vines brushed against the windscreen. The light became greyer as the heavy growth blocked out most of the sunshine. It was hard to believe they were only a few hundred yards off the highway, Elena thought, glancing over her shoulder at the seemingly impenetrable jungle behind them. She felt as if they had entered another world, one composed of heat, humidity, and the shrieking cries of unseen birds.

'Nobody's following us,' she said with a sigh of relief.

Blake nodded. 'Good. All we've got to worry about now is whether or not the car can take much more of this.'

The answer came quickly. The engine began to labour loudly as the car bucked like an unbroken horse across the ruts and grooves in the dirt. Elena braced her feet against the floor and her hands against the dashboard as the engine wheezed, gave a last gasping cough, and then spluttered into silence.

'Goddammit!' Blake slammed his hand against the steering wheel. 'Come on, baby,' he muttered. 'Don't give up now.' Elena held her breath as he turned the key and stepped on the accelerator. The engine cranked and caught, only to die seconds later. He sighed and threw open his door. 'Maybe something was jarred loose.'

'You mean maybe something wasn't,' Elena said, trying to take the edge off the situation. But Blake's face was grim as he opened the hood and peered into the engine.

'Nothing I can see,' he said finally. There was a moment's silence, and then he slammed his fist against the fender and uttered a string of curses that pinkened her ears.

She opened the door slowly and stepped outside. The heat of the jungle made the breath catch in her throat.

'Have we broken something?' she asked carefully.

He sighed and shook his head. 'It's my fault, Princess.'

The distress on his face made her heart go out to him. 'This road would kill any car, Blake. Didn't you just say you needed four-wheel drive...'

'Believe it or not, the road's not what did us in. It's the petrol I put into this thing.'

Elena shook her head. 'I don't understand.'

He walked to the rear of the car and opened the trunk. 'I was so damned glad to get my hands on some fuel that I never thought to check on what was coming out of that pump.' He pulled out a small, soft-sided valise, zipped it open, and dumped out the contents. 'Garbage,' he said as he stuffed handfuls of things back into it, 'that's what it was. The petrol is contaminated with water and God knows what.'

'But you had no way of knowing that. There was only the one pump...'

'...yes, and I probably sucked the bottom of it dry. How could I have been so stupid?' He shook his head and tossed the soft case at her. 'Here, put the stuff you bought into this. Just give me a minute or two...'

'Blake? Don't blame yourself for what happened.'

He sighed. 'Elena, I know you mean well, but...'

'We'd have broken down anyway. You said yourself we were running on empty. So if you hadn't filled the tank, we'd have come to a halt before now.'

He lifted his head and stared at her, and then his teeth flashed in a quick grin.

'Now, why didn't I remember that, Princess?'

Her smile matched his. 'Modesty forbids me telling you that you would have eventually,' she said.

Blake's eyes glinted with laughter. 'All right, woman. When your life depends on me thinking kindly of you, I'll remember that act of decency. Now, go on and pack that case. We have a lot of walking ahead of us.'

She leaned against the car and peered into the soft bag he'd tossed to her. 'The man's a walking supermarket,' she murmured. 'What did you put in here, Blake?' she called. 'Quinine—aspirin—bandages—antiseptic...' A hint of laughter wove into her voice. 'I don't suppose you have a couple of blankets stashed away, do you? We're liable to need them...'

Elena turned towards him, a smile on her face, and her words trailed away into silence.

Blake was standing beside the car, changing his clothes. A pair of faded blue jeans hung low on his lean hips; beneath, she caught a glimpse of dark briefs. He was pulling on an equally faded blue shirt, drawing it down over his tanned torso. Her gaze moved over the dark mat of hair that crossed his chest, then tapered to a narrow line as it bisected his muscled abdomen. His eyes met hers as he tugged the shirt into place and he smiled.

'Just give me a minute,' he said, tucking the shirt into his jeans. 'Let me pull on a pair of boots and I'll be ready for anything.'

Elena nodded. All she could think of was that she wished she could say the same.

Return this card **TODAY** to qualify for
the $1,000,000.00 Grand Prize **PLUS** a
Cadillac Coupe de Ville **AND** over
5000 other cash prizes!

If offer card is missing, write to: Harlequin Reader Service® 901 Fuhrmann Blvd P.O. Box 1867 Buffalo NY 14269-1867

NO POSTAGE
NECESSARY
IF MAILED
IN THE
UNITED STATES

BUSINESS REPLY MAIL
FIRST CLASS MAIL   PERMIT NO. 717   BUFFALO, NY

POSTAGE WILL BE PAID BY ADDRESSEE

HARLEQUIN
READER SERVICE®
MILLION DOLLAR SWEEPSTAKES
901 Fuhrmann Blvd.
P.O. Box 1867
Buffalo NY 14240-9952

DETACH ALONG DOTTED LINE

CHAPTER SEVEN

ELENA ran her fingers through her hair and shook her head wildly.

'Damn it,' she muttered, 'go on—get away from me!'

Blake looked up and grinned. 'Gnats,' he said. 'The terrors of the jungle.' He leaned into the trunk of the car and dug into the sack of supplies she'd bought at Las Palmas. 'Douse yourself with some of this,' he said, tossing her a can of repellent.

She depressed the button on the aerosol can and sprayed a bit on her hand.

'Whew,' she said, turning her face away from the pungent smell, 'that's awful!'

Blake nodded. 'Worse than awful,' he said agreeably. 'But it's all we've got. Go on, spray it on. Put some on your face, too.'

She made a face but she did as he'd asked, and then she tossed the can back to him.

'OK,' she said, 'no bug in its right mind will come near me now.'

'Until you begin to sweat that stuff off,' he said, ducking his head into the open trunk of the car again. 'Here,' he said as he straightened up, 'catch.'

A pale blue shirt came sailing through the air. Elena caught it and looked at him.

'What's this for?'

He barely looked up. 'Take off what you're wearing and put that on instead,' he said.

She looked at the shirt again. It was his, obviously, long-sleeved and made of cotton. It would hang to her knees, she thought, and the sleeves would dangle inches beyond her fingertips. All that extra fabric would be hot and bulky. Her own shirt was short-sleeved and scoop-necked.

'Thanks,' she said with a smile, 'but I'll stick with what I have on.'

'Change your shirt, Elena.'

Her smile wavered. Was there an edge to his voice? No, of course there wasn't. He'd told her she'd have to follow orders, but surely not about something as trivial as this.

'Look, I'm sure you mean well, Blake, but...'

His eyes met hers. 'Do it.'

'But it's silly. I...'

'I told you to do something, Elena. Now, do it!'

Disbelief clouded her features. He had to be joking— but he wasn't. His voice was hard as steel, and the look on his face...

'All right,' she said stiffly. 'Have it your way.'

She stepped behind the car and drew her shirt over her head. So, she thought, that's how it was going to be. Nothing would be trivial; Rogan was going to remind her of her vow to obey whenever he had the chance. A hot tide of anger raced through her. Her guard had slipped for a moment there and she'd almost thought he was human. But he wasn't; he was cold and heartless and a petty dictator...

And she was stuck with him. She slipped his shirt on and began to button it. What a pleasure it would be to reach Miami and be free to tell Blake Rogan exactly what she thought of him. And she'd tell her father, too. Whatever he'd paid for Rogan's services, it had been too much.

She grimaced as she looked down at herself. The shirt was even larger than she'd expected. It hung below her

knees and the sleeves were a hand's length too long. And
she was sweating already. She opened the first few
buttons, rolled the cuffs until they were at her elbows,
and stepped out into the road again.

'Satisfied?' she asked coolly.

Blake was looping a belt through the handles of the
carryall. He glanced at her and then went back to what
he was doing.

'Roll the sleeves down, Elena.'

Her jaw clenched. 'Aye aye, captain.'

He looked up again, his eyes narrowed. Her heart
thudded, but then he sighed.

'Look, Princess, it's going to be buggy as hell once
we start walking. And it's going to be hot. You'll
sweat...'

His tone was mild, but she was too angry to notice.
'I'm sweating already,' she said. 'This damned shirt is
too warm. It cuts off what little breeze there is. And...'

His mouth twisted in a wry smile. 'What it cuts off
are the bugs, Elena. The spray's going to wear off once
you start sweating, and then the bugs will start dropping
in for dinner. You want to offer them as little exposed
skin as possible, unless you like the idea of becoming a
walking buffet for everything that has wings.'

She felt a prickle of contrition. It was a reasonable
explanation, she thought, watching him stuff the carryall.
Maybe she'd over-reacted. Maybe this hadn't simply been
an exercise in command. But if it hadn't been, if he
simply wanted to keep her from being plagued by in-
sects, why had he made a simple situation so difficult?

Elena's eyes narrowed. Because it wasn't simple, that
was why. Because Rogan wanted to put her through her
paces, because he couldn't resist the chance to remind
her he was in charge, because he was the kind of man
he was...

'I can take care of myself,' she snapped.

He looked up and she drew in her breath. There was a measuring coldness in his eyes that made her wish she could call her words back. But it was too late for that, she thought, as the silence between them stretched on. Then, at last, he shrugged.

'Yes,' he said, his voice so low she had to strain to hear it, 'you sure as hell can.'

'Well, then, you...' A frown creased her forehead. 'What are you doing?'

It was a stupid question. She could see what he was doing—he was hoisting the improvised pack on his shoulder, sliding the machete into his belt, and marching off along the road, heading deeper into the jungle.

'Rogan? Rogan, don't you just walk away from me...' Her voice rose. 'Dammit, Rogan...' He was almost out of sight, swallowed by the heavy foliage. She took a step forward and then another. 'Rogan?' she said in a disbelieving whisper. He couldn't just leave her here—could he? Elena ran forward a few steps. 'Blake, please...'

This time, he stopped at once, his back to her. There was a tension in the set of his head and shoulders that made her skin prickle.

'What do you want, Elena?'

'Where...where are you going?'

There was a pause barely longer than a heartbeat. 'North. To the mountains.'

'On this road?'

He turned towards her slowly and lowered the carryall to the ground. 'Did you have a better idea?' he asked politely.

Too politely. 'Well, no,' she said, 'but...'

Blake nodded, his expression thoughtful. 'Elena,' he said softly, 'you have a decision to make. You can come with me, or you can stay here.'

Two spots of colour splashed across her cheeks. 'I just asked you a simple question, Blake. I thought...'

His eyes turned the colour of midnight. 'Don't,' he growled.

'Don't?'

'That's right—don't. Don't think. Don't question.' His hands went to his hips. 'That was the deal we made, remember?'

'Yes, but you can't expect me to...to just follow you blindly, no matter what you do or say or...'

His lips curved in a smile that never reached his eyes. 'You're right,' he said softly. 'I can't.'

In one fluid motion, he hoisted the carryall again, turned his back to her, and started walking briskly along the road.

Within seconds, the encroaching jungle had swallowed him up.

Elena stared at the empty road in disbelief. What kind of game was this? She took a hesitant step forward and then another. Come on, Rogan, she thought, get it over with. Step out on the road and bark an order at me...

But the road stretched ahead emptily. And gradually, as the silence settled around her, the sounds of the jungle returned. A bird screamed somewhere in the dark green canopy overhead.

Elena glanced over her shoulder at the narrow road that led to the highway. A brisk twenty-minute walk would take her back to it. Sure it would—and then she could choose between going back to the fighting in the south or heading north to the roadblock.

'Terrific,' she murmured aloud, and then she sighed. There was a third choice, and it was the only one she could make. She'd have to catch up to Rogan and eat humble pie.

She began walking along the narrow road. It stretched ahead like an arrow before curving to vanish in the encroaching tangle of trees. That was probably where Blake was waiting for her. Of course he'd wait for her, no matter what he threatened. After all, he'd had the chance to leave her behind before and he hadn't. Her footsteps slowed. Let him wait. Let him worry a little bit. It would do him good.

But he wasn't waiting in the curve of the road. She came around the bend and the road stretched on again until it lost itself in the green of the forest. It wasn't actually a road. Not any more. It was rutted and overgrown, dark beneath an overhanging canopy of leaves. Sweat dripped off the tip of Elena's nose into her mouth. She felt the light brush of something leggy on her cheek and she flinched as she brushed it away.

The bugs were impossible. Blake was right—they seemed to attack any unprotected inch of skin, and never mind the repellent. She grimaced and wiped her arm across her forehead. Sweat darkened her sleeve—*Blake's sleeve*—and she sighed. Maybe she owed him an apology about the shirt. Just maybe...

Something crashed through the underbrush and her heart skipped erratically. Soldiers, she thought. Or rebels. It had to be; there was no animal in the jungle large enough to make so much noise. Jaguars were large, yes, but the big cats never hunted this time of day. And animals moved through the heavy shrubbery without making a sound...

A troop of monkeys suddenly swung across the road ahead and Elena laughed aloud. Monkeys! Of course—she should have thought of that right away. Her father always said they were the noisiest creatures he knew.

'It's the jaguars and the anacondas that move like ghosts,' he'd told her when she was little and she curled up in his lap, demanding stories of the jungle.

And her mother would laugh and chide him. 'Don't frighten Elena,' she'd say. 'What does she know of jungles, Eduardo?'

It was true, she knew nothing of them. There was always a classmate or a teacher who'd ask her some wide-eyed question about jungle creatures, and then she'd have to explain that she lived in a modern ranch house just outside the capital city, and that she'd never been in a jungle in her life.

She'd never been in the midst of a revolution before, either. And now here she was, trapped in both. And she was alone. Alone—without Blake, without the man who'd kept her safe, who'd brought her all this distance. He could have abandoned her hours ago, but he hadn't. He'd stayed with her, protected her, held her in his arms...

'Change your mind, Princess?'

He was there, suddenly, standing before her as she came around a bend in the trail. She tried to stop in time but it was too late, and, as she stumbled forward, he caught her in his arms. She fell against him, leaning into his hard body, closing her eyes and savouring the feeling of relief that turned her legs to jelly. His heart beat smoothly and steadily beneath her ear.

'I thought...' She drew a deep breath. 'I thought you'd left me.'

His arms seemed to tighten around her. 'Isn't that the way you want it, Elena?'

There was a silence. 'No,' she said finally. Her face was pressed against his shirt. It was damp with his sweat, the taste of it salty on her parted lips. 'No,' she said again, and a tremor passed through her. She leaned back against his encircling arms and looked up at him. 'I want to stay with you, Blake.'

She knew the words had come out strangely—her voice had a breathless quality to it, as if she were saying something else. Her heart thudded once and then seemed to stop, waiting. His eyes, she thought, staring into them, his eyes were that midnight-blue they'd been that night on the terrace, just before he'd kissed her.

The world seemed to stand still, everything around them becoming exaggerated—the heat, the humidity, the intense scent of jungle wild flowers—all of it seemed larger than life. Something was going to happen, she thought wildly. Something...

And then, suddenly, Blake's hands slid to her shoulders and he pushed her from him.

'OK,' he said. His voice was hoarse, and he cleared his throat. 'OK. We'll give it another try.'

Elena nodded. She felt a strange kind of disappointment, as if something that had been just within her grasp had slipped away. But she smiled at him and, after a moment, he smiled back.

'I get a second chance, then,' she said.

He nodded. 'I know you think I'm being a hard-nosed bastard, but...'

She took a deep breath. 'Blake, were you waiting for me, or did you come back to look for me?'

His hands tightened on her shoulders. 'Does it matter?' She said nothing and finally he ran his tongue across his lips. 'I came back for you. But next time...'

His words sent a spiralling warmth through her body. 'Thank you,' she said softly.

A quick smile flickered on his mouth. 'You're welcome.' The smile faded and his hands fell to his sides. 'Look,' he said briskly, 'if we should run into real trouble, I can't afford to stand around and explain my decisions to you.' His eyes sought hers. 'Do you understand?'

Elena nodded. 'I think so.'

'I hope so. As it is, we've lost time. There's not a lot of daylight left, and we've got to make the most of it.' He opened the carryall and pulled out one of the bottles of beer she'd purchased in Las Palmas. 'Thirsty?'

'Parched. My throat's like sandpaper.'

White foam spewed from the bottle as he opened it and handed it to her. 'Drink up,' he said. 'Half for you, half for me.'

She closed her eyes with pleasure as the warm, bitter liquid spilled down her throat. After a few gulps, she handed the bottle to Blake, watching as he tilted it to his mouth and finished the beer. He grinned at her as he wiped his hand across his lips.

'Better?'

She nodded. 'Much.'

'OK,' he said, hoisting the makeshift pack on his shoulder again, 'let's move out. What we both need is a hot meal, a bath, and a soft bed.'

She laughed as she fell in beside him. 'Half a pint and the man's drunk.' They walked in silence for a few minutes and then she looked up at him. 'Blake, why haven't we seen anybody else along this road? I mean, is that good or bad?'

Blake shrugged. 'Good, I hope. I think it means we guessed right—that all the action's back there on the highway.'

'Yes, that makes sense. I just wonder...I wonder how long it will take to reach the mountains.' Elena glanced at the dark jungle on either side of the road. 'I guess we'll still be here by nightfall,' she said, trying to sound unconcerned.

'Maybe. But this trail's got to lead somewhere. What I'm hoping is that there's a village ahead.'

'And if there isn't?'

He shrugged again. 'If there isn't, Princess, we'll just have to do the best we can.'

They walked on in silence. Talking took energy—more than she had, Elena thought. And it invited the ever-present gnats to try for a landing in her mouth. She glanced at her watch. It was getting later and later. She was soaked with sweat; the wet, wonderful taste of the beer was only a memory. It was beginning to look as if they would still be here by nightfall—although even that idea was beginning to sound good. At least she could take off her sneakers and close her eyes and . . .

Blake grabbed her wrist. 'Smell that?' he asked. 'Do you know what it is?'

'Yes,' she said wearily. 'It's me. Between the sweat and the bug spray, I . . .'

Her words drifted into silence as a delighted smile spread across her face. What she smelled was woodsmoke. And it carried with it the scent of something delicious, something that made her stomach growl.

Blake laced his fingers through hers. 'Remember the hot meal I promised you, Princess?'

'Don't forget the bath,' she whispered as she followed him along a narrow trail that led off the road. 'And the soft bed . . .'

He grinned. 'There it is,' he said. 'It's not Santa Rosa, but it sure as hell looks pretty good to me.'

'Paradise,' Elena said, staring at the cluster of thatched huts that stood scattered in a clearing. She sniffed appreciatively. 'I just hope they're in the mood for guests.'

Blake laughed softly. 'How could anybody be less than thrilled with a couple as elegant as us? Come on, let's go. I made dinner reservations for seven and it's pushing towards that now.'

The village dogs discovered them before anyone else. Their excited barking brought the villagers from their huts, and soon they were surrounded by women in long, colourful skirts and men in pale cotton shirts and trousers. The Indians' smiles were polite but cautious, until Blake began to speak to them in the clicking Indio tongue. Shy smiles turned into grins of welcome and, within minutes, Elena and Blake had been invited to dinner and to stay the night.

'Where did you learn to speak that?' Elena murmured.

He shrugged modestly. 'I've been south of the border before.'

Of course he had, she thought, as the village men surrounded him. Men like Rogan had been travelling in these jungles for centuries, caught up in a never-ending search for gold, for precious gems, for the exotic and the exciting. Was that what she was? Was she an adventure, a story Blake would trot out on a cold winter's night for amusement? Would he have to search his mind for the name of the woman he'd once taken as his wife?

Blake's arm slid around her. 'Hey,' he whispered, 'why the long face, Princess?'

'I...I guess I'm just tired. And hungry.' Elena managed a smile. 'It's been a long day.'

His expression softened. 'Yes,' he said, 'I know it has. You'll feel better after you've eaten.'

The sun was sinking behind the trees by the time they'd finished a simple meal of chicken and yams, wrapped and baked in palm leaves. And Elena, who always thought of herself as a night person, was yawning.

Blake rose to his feet. 'Let me find out about the sleeping arrangements, Princess.'

Elena nodded and yawned again. She watched as he crossed the clearing and sought out the old woman who'd served them their meal. The woman peered up into his face as he spoke and then she said something. Blake answered and she gave him a toothless smile.

'OK, Princess,' he called, 'it's bedtime.'

They followed the old woman as she shuffled to a small hut on the far side of the clearing. She mumbled something to Elena, who smiled and shook her head.

'I don't understand her, Blake. What's she saying?'

'She's wishing us goodnight, Princess. Tell her "thank you".'

'Gracias, señora. Buenas noches.'

The woman patted her arm, said something that made Blake laugh, and then she scurried off.

Elena turned to Blake with a puzzled smile on her face. 'What was that all about?'

He grinned. 'You're not going to like it, Princess.'

'Come on,' she insisted as she followed him into the hut, 'tell me what she said.'

Blake shrugged. 'She assured me that many strong sons have been conceived in here.'

Elena's mouth fell open. 'What?'

He touched his finger to her mouth. 'You'll catch a mouthful of gnats,' he said, and then he laughed softly. 'It's the bridal suite, Princess. They had nothing else to offer.'

'You mean, you told her we were married? Rogan, you shouldn't have done that. You...'

Her words fell into silence as Blake's hands cupped her shoulders. The hut was cramped and dark, barely large enough for two. Suddenly, the laughter was gone.

'I told her the truth, Elena,' he said softly. She swallowed drily as his hands slid down her arms. 'We are married. And this is our wedding night.'

Her breath caught as their eyes met. Blake's pupils were as black and deep as shadowed pools. Elena swayed in his grasp. He was going to kiss her, she thought, and her heart hammered crazily. He was going to take her in his arms and kiss her and . . .

'Would you rather sleep outside, Elena?'

She nodded. 'Yes,' she said quickly.

His mouth twisted. 'It's not safer there, if that's what you're thinking.'

'I . . . I wasn't thinking anything. I mean, it'll be cooler, won't it? Outside . . .'

'But not safer.' Amusement danced in his eyes. 'Unless you're not worried about the vampire bats.'

Elena grasped his sleeve. 'What vampire bats? My father never mentioned vampire bats, and he camped at archaeological sites for years.'

Blake shrugged. 'Why would he have told you about them, Princess? It's not exactly a bedtime story for children, is it? But you don't have to be too concerned. They're not the way they're made out to be in films.' He smiled at her. 'The bats prefer horses to people. Well, that's if there are horses around. But they're willing to take a meal from somebody's big toe if that's what available.'

'You're making that up,' Elena said positively, but one look at his face told her he wasn't. 'All right, Rogan,' she said quickly, 'you've made your point. We'll sleep in here. You on that side of the hut,' she added firmly, pointing with her finger, 'and me on this side.'

Blake scuffed the mat with the toe of his boot. 'There's only one mat, Princess. Are you offering to give it up?'

She lifted her chin and stared at him. 'God, you're a perfect gentleman, aren't you?'

He grinned. 'I'm a man in need of a good night's sleep, sweetheart.'

She stared at him for a second and then her chin rose. 'Is there a place where I can wash?' she asked coolly. 'I'd like to scrub off some of this dirt.'

Blake grinned at her. 'After you, Princess,' he said, making a sweeping bow. 'Our hostess said the facilities are just up the trail.'

The facilities were a small spring that bubbled up from a rocky cairn. Elena watched as Blake unconcernedly pulled off his shirt, bunched it up and soaked it in the water. He scrubbed at his neck and shoulders, and then he ran the wet shirt across his chest. In the fading daylight, the muscled planes and ridges of his arms and torso looked as if they'd been touched with gold. When he opened the top button of his jeans, Elena blushed and turned away.

'Would you step behind a tree or something?' she asked stiffly. 'I . . . I'd like to get washed, too.'

He laughed softly. 'Of course, Princess. Forgive me. Modesty's such a nice quality in a bride. I'll see you at the hut.'

She said nothing while he moved off. After a moment, she unbuttoned her shirt—his shirt, she reminded herself—and knelt beside the spring. She eased the shirt off her shoulders, and then bent forward and cupped her hands in the water.

The cool sweetness of it made her gasp. Elena splashed the water over her face and dribbled it over her shoulders and breasts. Sighing with pleasure, she bent forward and let it spill over her hair. Perhaps there'd be time tomorrow for a real scrub, she thought, but for now, the water alone felt wonderful. She got to her feet and looked around her. It was almost dark and she was still alone. Quickly, she slipped off her sneakers and socks, unzipped her jeans and stepped free of them.

The air was still warm, and it felt like silk against her flesh. She stood there for a moment, wearing only a pair of cotton bikini underpants, and then she sighed and reached for the shirt. If only she had the courage to sleep in just the shirt, she thought, picking it up slowly. But at least she'd had the heavy jeans off for a little while. At least...

'Dammit, Elena, what the hell are you...'

She gasped as Blake stepped into the clearing. In that final moment before nightfall, he was visible only as a silhouette against the trees. He took a slow step forward and she felt a pulse begin to beat in her throat.

'I thought something had happened to you,' he said. His voice was thick and husky. 'I thought...'

'Blake, I didn't realise...' She stuffed her arms into the sleeves of the shirt and pulled it around her. Her hands trembled as she began to do up the buttons. 'I didn't realise I'd taken so long,' she said. 'Just let me...'

'Let me,' he said in that same thick voice. She stood still while he reached towards her, barely breathing while he buttoned the shirt. His hands brushed lightly across her breasts and she caught her breath.

'Blake...'

The word was a whisper. She swallowed as his hands closed on the collar of her shirt and drew her forward. She could feel the warmth of his breath on her face.

'Elena,' he said softly. 'Princess...'

He reached out and touched his hand lightly to her cheek. A tremor raced through her at the heated feel of his skin against hers. He whispered her name again and her head lifted, her eyes searching his. He bent to her slowly, slowly, until finally his mouth touched hers.

'Don't,' she murmured.

But her body betrayed her. She moved against him and his hand spread along her cheek, cupping her face, raising it to him, and all the while his mouth was on hers, tasting her, urging her to taste him in return, and she knew that she wanted the kiss to go on for ever. She wanted more—to touch him, to be touched, to beg him to teach her all the things that existed only in the shadows of her dreams. And then, without warning, he grasped her arms and put her from him.

'No,' she whispered, 'please...'

His hand brushed her cheek and she opened her eyes. The moon was rising above the trees. In its faint light she thought she saw a glimmer of sadness in his eyes.

'It's all right, Princess,' he said softly, 'I understand. It's been a long day.'

She wanted to tell him that he hadn't understood her plea at all. But, before she could speak, he swung her up into his arms and carried her to their hut. Inside, in the velvety darkness that wrapped her in its soft embrace, he lowered her gently to the sleeping mat. Elena waited, breathless in the silence of the jungle night, as Blake lay down beside her. His arm closed around her waist and he drew her against him. Her breathing quickened as she felt the heat of his bare chest press against her back, felt the roughness of his denim-clad legs against the naked flesh of hers. The pulse in his throat beat erratically against her temple as she nestled her head under his chin.

'Goodnight, Princess,' he whispered. His lips touched her hair, and then everything was still.

CHAPTER EIGHT

MAZATAL. The name of the town almost a day's walk from the Indian village sounded magical. Elena had imagined an exotic city rising from the dark green of the rainforest with ancient Mayan majesty. What she found was a miserable collection of unpaved streets, adobe shacks, and scrawny dogs which lay slumbering in the afternoon heat, beneath the brooding splendour of the Mountains of the Moon. Their trek through the jungle had ended.

'It looks OK,' Blake said after a moment. 'I don't think the fighting's reached here yet.'

Elena sighed. 'I want a hot bath,' she said. 'And a cold drink. And . . .'

Blake grasped her wrist. 'Wait.'

'For what? There's nothing happening—you just said so. And I . . .'

One look at his face silenced her, and she sank to the ground beside him, her back pressed to the trunk of a tree. Blake squatted on his haunches beside her, staring down into the town. Elena followed his gaze, and suddenly realised that there was a flurry of activity in the town square.

'Troops?' she whispered.

He shook his head. 'No,' he said finally, 'not troops.' He smiled and got to his feet. 'We're in luck. It's fiesta time in Mazatal.'

Elena rose and took his outstretched hand. 'They're putting up the banners in the plaza now. It's four o'clock,

113

Princess. Siesta's over and people are pouring into the square.'

'We're going to look awfully out of place for a festival,' Elena said as she looked down at her stained and ripped clothing. 'I thought the idea was not to draw attention to ourselves.'

'We won't if we get into the crowd and keep moving.' Blake smiled down at her upturned face. 'We'll be all right, Elena,' he said softly. 'I promise.'

By the time they'd scrambled down the hillside, the streets of the little town were filled. Blake slid his arm around Elena's waist and they moved into a crowd. No one gave them a second glance, except for one man whose dark glance swept over Elena's tousled hair and stained clothes. But when Blake's eyes locked with his, the stranger's face paled. He touched his hand to his hat and murmured something which Blake acknowledged with a curt nod.

Elena glanced up at the man beside her. The confrontation had been silent but impressive. No wonder the *campesino* had backed down, she thought. There was a dark, dangerous look about Blake, as if he belonged in this wild, untamed town. His hat was drawn down over his eyes, as it had been when they first met. A two-day beard shadowed his cheeks and jaw, and there was an unlit cheroot clamped in his teeth. His shirt was damp and clung tightly to his muscled shoulders and torso, and his jeans were moulded to his narrow hips and long legs. He was, she thought suddenly, every man's fear and every woman's desire. Her blood began to pulse swiftly in her throat.

Blake looked down at her and smiled. 'What's going through that pretty head of yours now, Princess?'

She blushed and looked away. 'I . . . I was just wondering where all these people came from,' she said. 'I mean, Mazatal's in the middle of nowhere.'

A child raced into the street ahead of them, a yapping dog at its heels, and collided with Blake's legs. The little boy went down in a tangle of limbs, his face contorting, but before he could cry, Blake scooped him into his arms and swung him high into the air.

'*Guardete, niño,*' he said, laughing as the boy's round, black eyes widened. 'You could get hurt in all this traffic.'

He set the giggling child down on the pavement and clasped Elena's hand in his. 'Amazing, isn't it? Fiesta time brings everybody in from miles around. Don't tell me that a little girl who grew up in San Felipe never went to a fiesta.'

'Only the ones in Santa Rosa. And they weren't like this.'

Blake laughed as they stepped around a group of Indians painted, from head to toe, with stripes of white and brown clay.

'No, I'll bet they weren't.'

Elena was peering over her shoulder. 'Blake?' she whispered. 'Those men had tattoos on their faces.'

'They're probably *Xivera* Indians.' He drew her closer to him and put his lips to her ear. 'Headhunters,' he whispered.

Elena stared up at him. 'You're teasing me,' she said.

Blake grinned. 'Well, they were, twenty or thirty years ago.' He watched her wide eyes as she tried to take in the profusion of sights, and then he took her hand in his. 'Come on, Princess,' he said. 'We'll take a quick trip through the market, buy what we need, and then we'll join the party.'

She looked up at him. 'Really?'

He touched his finger to her mouth and nodded. 'Really,' he said gently. 'We might as well enjoy ourselves.'

Elena stood before the cracked mirror in her hotel room, brushing her hair. It was still damp, and the ends curled softly on her shoulders. She'd soaked in the tub for an hour, until the water, none too hot to start with, had cooled and chilled her skin. She smiled at her reflection.

'You'll never be able to get us rooms,' she'd whispered to Blake as they stood inside the crowded entrance to Mazatal's only hotel.

But he'd done more then get them rooms, she thought, securing her hair behind her ears with tortoiseshell combs. He'd got her the only room with its own bath.

'The Honeymoon Suite,' he'd said with a grin as he handed her the key.

Her heart had seemed to stop while she'd waited for him to tell her they were sharing it. But his smile had twisted suddenly and he'd turned away from her. When he'd spoke, his voice had been brusque.

'I'll meet you downstairs at seven, Elena,' he'd said, and a strange hollow feeling expanded in her chest as she'd watched him stride away.

She put down the brush and turned to the bed. Blake had bought her an armful of clothing at the market—things for the mountains, he'd said, while she selected sneakers and jeans and shirts. And then, without asking her opinion on colour or style, he'd carefully chosen a blouse, skirt, shawl, and leather sandals for her to wear this evening.

'This one,' he'd said, almost gruffly, handing her a cream-coloured blouse woven of cotton so soft and fine that it had the substance of a spider's web. 'And that,' he'd added, pointing to a black skirt with masses of red roses at the hem and waist.

Elena hadn't had the heart or the courage to tell him the outfit wasn't to her taste. The blouse was too plain, the skirt too gaudy. She sighed as she slipped the blouse over her head. It settled like gossamer over her shoulders, clinging lightly to her breasts. She looked at her reflection in surprise. There was nothing plain about the blouse; she was amazed she'd ever thought so. There was a delicate pattern of tiny flowers in it, roses, she realised, like the ones on the skirt. Her skin glowed golden against the creamy cotton.

She picked up the skirt, stepped into it, and looked at herself again. A slow smile curved along her mouth. The skirt was soft and feminine, fitting closely from waist to hip and then flaring gently until it was a mass of heavy folds that ended just below the knee. Elena turned slowly, watching as the skirt whirled softly away from her bare legs. The outfit was simple and in quiet good taste, yet it emphasised the provocativeness of her slender body. Her skin tingled as she imagined Blake's face when he saw her.

Suddenly, she remembered another evening when she'd stood before a mirror, staring at her reflection. She had been on the threshold of puberty, but there was no one to tell her about the mysteries her body would undergo on its way to womanhood. She had been looking into the mirror as she changed for dinner, and had been transfixed by her own image. Margarita, the ascetic housekeeper who'd believed that fasting was good for the soul, had come upon her just as Elena lightly touched her newly burgeoning breasts.

'Look, Margarita,' she'd said with innocent wonder, 'I'm becoming a woman.'

The housekeeper had grasped her wrists roughly and pulled her hands to her sides.

'Stop that, *niña*,' she'd hissed. 'Believe me, it is best to remain a child as long as you may.'

And then she'd told her all about men, about the things they wanted of a woman's body. Elena's face had whitened.

'But...but why?' she'd whispered. 'Why would a woman let anyone do those things to her?'

Margarita had grimaced. 'It is a duty, *niña*. But there is no pleasure in it.'

There had been no other talk of sex. 'You know all about that sort of thing, don't you, darling?' her mother had asked once, just before Elena had turned thirteen. Embarrassment had made Elena nod her head. In boarding-school, the other girls' giggled and whispered conversations after lights-out made her suspect that there might be more to it than Margarita had told her. Eventually, Elena had come to believe that what happened between men and women was terribly overrated and not worth all the attention the world seemed to give it. It might even be pleasant, as Jeremy's soft goodnight kisses sometimes were...

Heat and apprehension flooded through her as she remembered the taste of Blake's mouth and the feel of his hands on her body. The fiery excitement of his touch had shocked her. Never, except in the hidden depths of a dark dream, had her flesh quickened before. And when his hands had brushed her breasts—even the memory made her nipples tighten and ache...

Elena turned quickly from the mirror and snatched up the shawl Blake had bought her. He was not the villain she'd thought him to be, that much was true. He had a sense of honour; he could have abandoned her at any time in the past days and he hadn't. But he was still an adventurer perennially in search of an elusive pot of gold. It was why her father had been able to buy his services. And once he'd brought her safely to Miami, he'd be off chasing another rainbow.

She tossed her head and took a deep breath. 'You've got jungle fever, Elena Teresa,' she said aloud. But her voice lacked conviction, and she had to pause at the door and rest her forehead against the cool adobe wall before she could trust herself to leave the room.

Her new sandals slapped softly against the wooden stairs as she went swiftly downstairs. The little hotel was crowded; people brushed by her as she went through the lobby to the rear courtyard where dinner was being served. She hesitated as she stepped out into the cobblestoned courtyard. It was crowded with tables and chatting diners; candles flickered and a guitar played softly in the background. Her glance went from table to table. Everyone was dressed for fiesta. The dark-eyed women glowed and the men were handsome in the tall, dark way many of them were in this northern province. But none had hair the colour of chestnuts and eyes the colour of the sky.

The weakness trembled within her again, and Elena closed her eyes. 'Stop it,' she whispered to herself.

'I can't,' a deep voice said just beside her. 'I always get this foolish look on my face when I see a beautiful woman.'

Her eyes flew open and she stared into Blake's face. He was standing beside her, smiling down at her, and the breath caught in her throat when she looked at him. How beautiful he was, she thought. He was wearing white linen trousers that fitted him snugly, and a dark brown shirt, the top buttons left undone so that the golden column of his throat was exposed. His thick, dark hair was still damp, as if he'd just come from the shower.

He'd shaved, too, and the smoothness of his skin made his eyes seem even more blue than she remembered.

He smiled into her eyes. 'Good evening, Princess,' he said softly.

Elena cleared her throat. 'Good . . . good evening,' she murmured. 'You look . . .' She swallowed hard. 'You look . . . nice.'

Blake's smile softened. 'Thank you, Princess. You look nice, too.'

She looked up at him quickly, half expecting to see that glint of cool amusement she'd seen in his eyes in the past, but he was smiling at her with quiet solemnity.

'Shall we go in to dinner?'

She nodded and he took her arm, leading her across the courtyard to a candlelit table near a bank of gloriously blooming poincianas. Was it her imagination, or were the other diners watching them? No, she thought, it was true. She dismissed the appraising looks of the men: she was Spanish enough to know that Latin men always measured an unknown woman. It was the women who surprised her. They were watching Blake from beneath their lashes, and she realised, with a sudden swell of pride, that they envied her for having a man like him at her side, envied the possessive curve of his arm around her waist and the intimate smile meant for her alone. She looked up at him as he pulled a chair out for her. Their eyes met, and her heart began to race.

'Thank you,' she said.

Blake slid into the chair opposite her. 'You're welcome, Princess. I hope you don't mind—I've already ordered for both of us.'

Elena smiled. 'Don't tell me you're asking me for my opinion, Mr Rogan,' she said softly.

He sighed. 'I don't suppose we could declare a truce tonight, could we?'

The hint of a smile curved across her lips. 'I was only teasing, Blake. Actually, I owe you an apology.'

'An apology?' Elena nodded. 'Am I going to be able to take this on an empty stomach, Princess? This sounds pretty serious.'

'It is serious. If we'd taken a vote each time a decision had to be made, we'd still be on the road outside Las Palmas. I'm sorry I didn't understand that. You've been right from the beginning.'

Blake laughed softly. 'I think I must be hearing the sweet voice of Elena Teresa Maria Consuelo Esteban. She's the one your father promised me, you know.'

'When he... when he made his proposition to you, you mean?'

There was the faintest of pauses. 'Yes, that's right. He told me you'd been raised as a proper *señorita* should be.' He smiled at her as the waiter poured their wine. 'He never told me you were harbouring a firebrand named Elena Kelly inside you, Princess.'

She smiled at him in return. 'Well, even the Kellys admit when they're wrong. I should have said it sooner, Blake, but...'

'But you're stubborn.'

She laughed. 'Of course. How else would anyone know that the blood of the Irish runs in my veins?'

Blake's eyes darkened. 'I knew it, Princess, as soon as I saw that your eyes were the colour of the sea in winter, as soon as I felt the silkiness of your skin...'

'Con permiso, señorita.'

Elena's eyes slid from his and fixed on the table. The waiter was putting a plate before her, but she had no idea what was on it. Colours, textures, everything was a blur. Her hand trembled as she reached for her glass. She took a sip and then forced a smile to her face.

'What about you?' she asked.

'We were talking about you, Princess.'

'Exactly. We never talk about you, Blake. I don't know anything about you.'

A lazy smile stole across his face. 'Not so, Princess,' he said softly. 'You know a lot about me. You know that I sleep on my right side, that I never snore, that your body fits against mine like the last piece of a jigsaw puzzle.'

Elena felt as if someone had touched the candle flame to her cheeks. 'Don't tease me, Blake. I...'

'When I awoke this morning, you were lying in the curve of my arm, with your head on my shoulder and your hand on my chest.' He looked into her eyes and his voice dropped to a husky whisper. 'Did you sleep well, Elena? You bolted from the hut before I had a chance to ask.'

No, she thought, she hadn't bolted, she'd fled for her life when she'd awoken and found herself curled in Blake's arms, with him smiling down at her and his breath warm on her skin.

'I... I slept very well,' she said stiffly. 'Did you?'

She wanted to call the naïve question back as soon as she'd asked it, but it was too late. Blake grinned at her.

'No, not as well as I might have,' he said. He sighed as a blush spread across her face. 'What am I going to do with you, Princess? When you look at me like that, I feel guilty as hell for teasing you.'

'You can make up for it,' she said quickly. 'You can tell me something about yourself.'

He sat back and pushed his plate aside. 'OK,' he said, 'what do you want to know?'

Everything, she thought, but she caught herself in time. 'Well, where are you from? What part of the States?'

He pulled the box of cheroots from his shirt pocket and took one out. 'Philadelphia.'

Elena's eyes widened. 'Philadelphia?'

'Philadelphia,' he repeated. 'Why?'

She put her hand to her mouth, but it was impossible to stifle her soft laughter. 'God, I'm sorry. It's just that— I don't know, I expected you to say something like...like Houston or Chicago. Philadelphia's so...so dignified and proper and...'

'And I'm not.' Blake laughed at the expression on her face. 'It's all right, Princess, I couldn't agree more. That's why I took off.'

'Took off?'

He nodded. 'I was twenty-one years old and I felt as if the city was choking me to death. So I opened a world atlas, closed my eyes, and stabbed my finger at a spot on a page.' He looked at her and grinned. 'Don't look so horrified, Princess. I'm exaggerating. Actually, I chose Belize rather carefully.'

'Belize? What's in Belize?'

Blake tapped the ashes from the cheroot into an ash tray. 'Copra, cedar, swamps and smugglers. All a man's heart could desire.' He looked at her and smiled. 'It was a hell of a lot more interesting than Philadelphia.'

Elena's eyes met his. 'Yes,' she said softly, 'I figured that. But you didn't stay in Belize.'

He shook his head. 'Nope. I tried Somalia next. And then Singapore, I think.' He grinned again. 'It's a long time ago, Princess. I can't really remember where I went next.'

'Didn't you ever find a place you liked?'

Blake shrugged his shoulders. 'I found lots of places I liked. But I wasn't looking for one to settle in.'

She took a breath. 'And...and you never married?'

He laughed softly. 'Hell, Princess, the life I live is no life for a woman.'

Elena nodded. He was only confirming everything she'd suspected. Then why was there a sudden constriction in her throat?

'So,' she said finally, 'you're the sort who wants what's over the next hill.'

'My father's words, exactly,' he said, giving her a quick smile.

'And what happens when you run out of hills?'

'You and my father would get along well, Princess,' Blake said. 'He asked me the same question. It was just before I left for Belize—I'd turned down the job he'd found for me, you see, and . . .'

'And what did you tell him?' she asked softly.

Blake shrugged his shoulders. 'I said I'd worry about that when the time came. Look, we've talked about me long enough. We . . .'

'Wasn't your mother upset when you left home?'

He lifted his glass and drank the last of his wine. 'I didn't exactly leave home, Princess. They asked me to go.'

Her eyes widened. 'They? Your parents, you mean?' He nodded, and she reached across the table and took his hand. 'Oh, Blake, that's awful. How could they do that?'

The vertical lines she'd seen before appeared between his eyebrows. 'Do what, Elena?'

'Throw you out,' she said indignantly. Her fingers laced through his and she leaned towards him. 'I'd never do that,' she said. 'I'd never throw you out, no matter what you'd done.'

His hand tightened around hers. 'Wouldn't you?' he asked softly.

Colour flooded her cheeks. 'N...no,' she stammered, 'of course not. Mothers shouldn't...'

A mischievous grin lit his face. 'Do you have maternal feelings towards me, Princess?'

Elena pulled her hand free of his. 'You're teasing me again,' she said lifting her chin.

Blake sighed. 'I apologise.' He waited until she gave him a tremulous smile and then he smiled in return. 'Now it's your turn. What's it like to live in Miami? Tropical nights on the beaches, dancing till dawn in the big hotels...' He laughed as she shook her head. 'No? You mean, it's not all palm trees and orange groves?'

She smiled. 'I work for my living, Blake. Don't look at me that way. I really do.'

'Elena Kelly speaking, hmm?'

Her smile broadened. 'Yes, exactly. And at the end of the day, I go back to my apartment—furnished efficiency, but with a marvellous view of the ocean. And I make myself dinner and curl up with a book and...'

'Where's Jeremy while all this is going on?'

Elena blinked. 'Jeremy?'

'Jeremy. Don't tell me your fiancé lets you spend your evenings alone.'

Fiancé... Dear heaven, why had she told him that stupid lie?

'Blake, about Jeremy...'

'In fact, why did he let you go to San Felipe by yourself? Everyone knew there was going to be trouble here.'

'He...he asked me not to go,' she said. It was true, Jeremy had suggested she stay in Florida. It would be safer, he'd said.

Blake's mouth hardened. '*Asked* you not to go? He should have *told* you not to go.'

'I make my own decisions. Jeremy...'

His eyes narrowed in speculation. 'He's a nice, safe choice, isn't he?'

Elena's eyebrows rose. 'And just what does that mean?'

He shrugged. 'It means he lets you do whatever you want to do, whenever you want to do it. It means he doesn't really expect more than you give him. It means...'

'He's not a petty dictator,' she said, her eyes meeting his.

Blake smiled wryly. 'Do you love him?'

She drew a deep breath. 'Why do you ask?'

He shrugged. 'I guess it's because I can't imagine you with a man like that. He sounds pale and spineless.'

Her chin lifted in defiance. 'Just because you don't understand Jeremy doesn't mean...'

'I asked you a question, Princess. Do you love him?'

Elena let out her breath. 'That's the reason people usually get engaged, isn't it?'

His teeth flashed in a quick smile. 'I wouldn't know. Getting engaged is like the bubonic plague—it's something I've managed to avoid so far.'

Elena flushed. 'Yes, I can imagine.'

Suddenly, he leaned across the table and his eyes bored into hers. 'I wouldn't have let my woman go off to San Felipe alone.'

Suddenly, the heat of the tropic night was unbearable. Elena felt as if she were struggling to breathe. In one quick motion, she pulled her hand free of his and got to her feet.

'Thank you for dinner,' she said. 'But it's getting late...'

Blake uncoiled from his chair and rose beside her. 'You're right, it is.' His arm slid around her waist. 'And I promised to show you the fiesta.'

She shook her head as he led her to the rear of the cobblestoned courtyard. It was darker here, away from the candlelit tables. The single guitar had been joined by another, and several couples were dancing to the softly romantic music.

'No, it's too late. You said we had to get an early start tomorrow.'

He trapped her in his arms. 'We have time for one dance, Elena. Stop fighting me and relax.'

'I don't want to dance. I...'

His arms tightened around her and he drew her against him. 'Shut up,' he said softly, and with a sigh of resignation, she did as he'd ordered.

He could force her to dance, but he couldn't force her to enjoy it, she told herself as they moved slowly around the courtyard. Her resolve was strong, and it worked—for a little while. But slowly, the plaintive melody of the guitar began to seep into her blood, and the heat of Blake's body began to warm hers, and she felt her tension easing away.

She closed her eyes and put her head against his chest. 'That's it,' he murmured. 'Just relax, Princess. Let yourself go.'

But that was just what she couldn't do. If she did ... if she did, she'd be lost. A tremor raced through her as she felt Blake's lips touch her hair.

'Elena.'

His voice was soft. She lifted her head from his chest to look up at him. She could still hear the guitar, playing faintly in the distance, but somehow, as they danced, Blake had led her from the courtyard and into the darkness. His arms were tight around her, holding her against the hardness of his body. She could see his eyes glinting in the moonlight, see the shadowed planes of his face. He said her name again and bent towards her, and as his mouth touched hers she closed her eyes and gave herself up to the moment.

She felt the touch of his mouth on hers, felt his hands moving up her spine until they were tangled in her hair as he lifted her face to his. His lips teased hers with soft, gentle kisses, that gradually changed, deepened, until she could feel his hunger for her. She whimpered against his mouth as his lips parted hers for the first passionate thrust of his tongue. Her hands moved up his arms to his shoulders, and she wound her arms around his neck, burying her fingers in his hair, loving the thick, wild feel of it against her skin.

'Elena, *mia amante...*'

Her head fell back as Blake's lips pressed against her neck, warming the tender skin behind her ear, then trailing moistly down her taut flesh until his mouth reached the hollow between neck and shoulder where her blood pulsed frantically. His hands slid down her back to her buttocks and he drew her up to him, until she was standing on tiptoe, until she could feel the hard, driving maleness of him pressing against her, telling her of his need and desire.

'Oh, God,' she said, not knowing whether her whisper was a plea for help or a prayer of thanks. Her heart was pounding, leaping as Blake's hands slipped beneath her blouse and cupped her breasts. The touch of his fingers against her nipples almost drove her to her knees. No one had ever touched her before, and yet Elena felt her flesh bloom and bud like a desert flower that had waited for his caressing palms to bring it to life.

'Elena, my wife...'

His wife. Yes, she thought as his mouth and hands brought fire to her blood, yes, she was his wife. There was nothing to stop them from going to her room, to

her bed, and finishing what had begun that day at the
market in Santa Rosa.

'Elena,' he whispered, his hands hot against her,
'Elena, come to me, come to me...'

And she would have, she knew that later when she lay
alone in her bed, still trembling with an intensity of an
emotion that she'd never dreamed existed. She would
have let him take her, there the darkness of the per-
fumed night, with the gui g sadly in the distance.

But suddenly there e sound of drunken
laughter. Elena e's embrace just as
a group of re e towards them, their raucous
voices cutting ugh the darkness. Blake cursed harshly
and reached out to her.

'Princess, wait...'

But she had fled.

CHAPTER NINE

At six in the morning, the dusty streets of Mazatal were deserted except for a pair of snoring *campesinos* who lay sprawled against the ▓▓ of the *cantina*, an empty bottle of *tequila* nestle▓ ▓▓ ▓▓ them. Blake stepped over them, lit a chero▓ ▓▓ ▓ the match aside.

'Wait here,' he said, bare▓ ▓▓ ▓▓ his shoulder.

Elena nodded. His words were cu▓ ▓is voice hard, as they'd been ever since he'd knocked on her door an hour earlier to awaken her. Not that she'd been asleep, she thought, watching his scowling face as he peered up the dusty street. She'd hardly closed her eyes all through the endless night.

But in the pre-dawn darkness, the light tap at the door startled her. She sat up quickly, clutching the blanket to her.

'Yes? Who's there?'

'Blake. We're leaving in an hour.'

The clipped words fell like blows. 'All right,' she'd answered, staring at the door as if she could see him through it. 'I'll be ready.'

She heard the sound of something hitting the floor, and then he spoke again. 'I'm leaving the carryall. Pack your things and meet me downstairs.'

She nodded foolishly, listening while his footsteps faded, and then she rose and dressed in the cotton trousers and shirt Blake had bought her yesterday, deliberately concentrating on nothing but the long day ahead.

They could be in Mexico a couple of days, if their luck held. Elena opened the door and took the carryall from the hallway. And then it would be over. She'd say goodbye and thanks to Blake Rogan and then she could try to forget these past days and...

Her fingers closed on the top item in the carryall. It was the brown shirt Blake had worn last night. Before she realised it, Elena lifted the shirt to her face and pressed it to her lips. It smelled of Blake, of his clean skin and male muskiness and the cheroots he smoked.

She sank on to the bed, still clutching the shirt. Forget these past days? No, she thought, burying her face in the soft fabric, no, she'd never do that. She'd never forget any of it—not after last night.

When she'd left the courtyard, Blake had followed her and stood outside the closed door of her room.

'Elena,' he'd said quietly, 'open the door.' But she'd stood silently in the dark, her forehead bowed against the warped wood of the door, breathing heavily, exhausted by an nameless inner turmoil. 'Princess, please, let me in.' Still she'd said nothing. When he spoke again, his voice was rough. 'All right, Elena, if that's the way you want it...'

As his angry footsteps had clattered down the steps, Elena had almost pulled open the door and told him that what she wanted was to be in his arms, but standing there in the dark, confused by the intensity of her emotions, she had been sure of only one thing. Her life would never be the same again if Blake made love to her.

The morning heat was beginning to weigh down on the quiet streets of Mazatal. Elena's gaze swept over Blake as he flung the stub of the cheroot to the ground and stamped it into the dust. Breakfast—fruit, bread and coffee—had been eaten in silence. Over strong black coffee, he'd tersely informed her that he'd managed to rent them a truck. Not much of a truck, he'd added, but it would speed their journey through the Mountains of the Moon.

'The sooner we reach Mexico, the better,' he'd said, and Elena had nodded in agreement. What she needed, she told herself, was to put this strange interlude quickly behind her. Everything would be all right then.

She looked up as a loud horn blasted the early morning silence. An ancient pick-up truck was rattling up the centre of the street towards them, glowing beneath a paint scheme that seemed to use all the primary colours. Blake walked towards it as it groaned to a stop.

'It's damned well about time,' he growled. 'Where the hell have you been, Manuel? You were supposed to be here at six sharp.'

A plump little man jumped from the cab, gold teeth gleaming in his apologetic smile. 'I am sorry, *señor*. I sleep late. Too much—how you say, *tequila, sí*?'

Blake pulled a stack of bills from his pocket and stuffed them into the man's hand. 'Yeah, well you can buy yourself lots more with this. Is the truck filled up?'

The little man nodded. '*Sí.* And I check the oil, as you ask.' He turned to Elena and beamed at her. '*Buenos días.*'

Elena nodded. '*Buenos días.*' She walked to Blake's side and stared at the truck. Its fenders were painted bright red, the hood blue, and the body yellow. But not even the garish paint could cover the rust beneath. 'The truck's older than I am,' she said under her breath.

'Is that a complaint, *señorita*?' Blake asked in a cold voice.

She paled. 'No, of course not. I only meant...'

He stared at her and then he let out his breath. 'Never mind, Elena. I know what you meant. Believe me, I didn't have any choice. It was this or nothing. Go on,' he said with a tight smile, 'get in. Manuel swears this thing runs better than it looks.'

'You will leave my truck with my cousin Teodoro in Galindo, yes?' the little man asked nervously as Blake gunned the engine to life. His voice rose above the labouring roar. 'The little house by the *cantina...*'

'...with the television antenna and the big brown dog. Yes, don't worry, Manuel. I'll leave it there.' Blake released the brake, stepped on the accelerator, and the truck jerked away from the hotel, the gears whining ominously. 'That's if we get that far,' he muttered as they rolled down the street in a series of neck-snapping stops and starts.

As they picked up speed, the truck seemed to shake itself free and, by the time they'd left Mazatal behind, they were moving along at a steady pace, with only an occasional rumble and jolt to remind them of the vehicle's age. But a new sound had been added, a musical tinkling that came from beneath the seat. Elena reached down and felt along the floor, and her fingers closed on a bottle.

'*Tequila,*' she said, holding it out for Blake to see.

His lips curved upward as the tinkling sounds continued. 'Several bottles, from the sound of it. Manuel's private stock, I guess. He's going to be mad as hell when he realises he forgot it.'

Elena returned the bottle to the cache beneath her seat and cleared her throat. 'The—er—the truck runs pretty well,' she said carefully.

He nodded. 'Yeah.'

She watched as he dug a cheroot from his pocket, stuck it between his teeth, and then struck a match between the thumb and forefinger of one hand. Silence stretched between them.

'Er—how far does this road go?' she asked finally.

Blake shrugged. 'Manuel says it crosses the border just past Galindo.'

She waited for him to say something more, but he didn't. They were leaving the valley now, beginning the climb into the Mountains of the Moon. Dark forest stood on either side of the narrow road as it curved its way upward. The gears squealed and grated as Blake changed down, and the engine began to labour, as if such hard work were more than it could handle. But Elena was aware only of the tension-filled atmosphere. She glanced at Blake, silently willing him to say something. When he didn't, she cleared her throat.

'How far is it from Galindo to the border?'

'An hour's walk, according to Manuel. We had quite a chat in the *cantina* last night.' He gave her a hard, quick glance. 'I didn't feel much like sleeping.'

Elena felt colour rise to her cheeks. 'Blake,' she said quickly, 'about last night . . .'

'What about it?'

'I . . . I'd like to explain . . .'

His teeth clamped tightly on the cheroot. 'You don't owe me any explanations.'

'But I do. I . . .'

'You don't have to worry. Our deal's still on. I'll get you to Miami.'

'I never thought you wouldn't. I . . . I was just thinking of how much better we'd been getting along, and . . .'

'Listen,' he said sharply, 'stop trying to dance around it. We made a mistake, that's all. We were both tired, we'd had some wine . . .' He glanced at her and then away. 'That's the way it was, wasn't it?'

No, she thought, no that's not the way it was for me . . . But admitting that would only make things more confused than they already were.

'Yes,' she said stiffly, 'that's the way it was.'

'Yeah,' he said softly, 'that's the way it was.' He rubbed the back of his neck. 'Like I said, forget it. We've got a long, hard day facing us.'

'Right.' Elena waited for a few minutes, but he said nothing more and the silence began to pool around them again. She ran her tongue over dry lips. 'It's not as hot as yesterday, is it? But then, it's almost the rainy season. This morning, I thought I smelled rain in the air, and...'

Blake changed down again as the grade steepened. 'Why don't you get some rest?' he said abruptly. 'We've got a long drive ahead.'

...and I don't want to hear you babbling like a fool. He hadn't said it, but he might as well have. Elena blinked back a sudden prickle of tears.

'Good idea,' she said in a voice that gave away nothing. 'Wake me when we get to Galindo.'

She lay her head back against the ripped upholstery and turned her head to the side, staring out at the dark forest without actually seeing it. Blake was right. It was better to pretend she was asleep than to go through hours of stilted conversation. Besides, if she kept talking, sooner or later she'd end up trying to explain why she'd run from him last night, and she couldn't very well do that, not when she didn't really understand the reason herself.

What she had to do was think about something else. Think about... about the art gallery. Or Jeremy. He'd be glad to see her. She'd phone him first thing, right after she phoned her father. Elena blinked her eyes. Was her father safe? God, but she hoped he was! She...

She cried out as the truck braked abruptly. She was catapulted forward, but Blake threw his arm across her before she could crack her head. The acrid smell of burned rubber filled the air as the brakes squealed and the truck came to a bone-jarring halt.

'What's the matter?'

'I'm not sure,' he muttered. 'There's a downed tree across the road, just around that curve, see it? Where the road goes through that ravine...'

Elena nodded. She could see only a piece of the trunk but it was enough to make her heart sink.

'It must have come down during a storm—it looks awfully big. I hope we'll be able to move it.'

Blake reached for the door-handle. 'I'll take a look.'

'I'll come with you. Maybe...'

His hand closed over hers as she reached for the door. 'No,' he said sharply. 'You stay here and keep your eyes and ears open.'

The skin along the back of her neck prickled. 'But Blake...'

He gave her a quick smile. 'I'll check things out. It's probably nothing more than it seems to be, Elena.'

Her throat had gone dry. 'And if it isn't?'

Blake's eyes met hers. 'If it isn't, I want you to get out of this truck and run like hell. You'd never be able to turn the truck on a road this narrow.'

'You think it's trouble, don't you? Tell me the truth, Blake. I have a right to know.'

'I just want to be sure, that's all. Hell, trees fall all the time, Princess.'

Her eyes searched his. 'You're lying,' she whispered. 'I know it.'

'Just sit tight and watch me. If I spot anything funny— that's *if*, Princess—I'll just come on back here and we'll figure another way to get to Galindo.'

'Blake, please, let's just go back now. We can...'

His fingers curled tightly around hers. 'But, if something does happen, get out of here fast. And don't look back until you reach Mazatal.'

Fear had turned her lips and tongue to cotton. 'I won't leave you,' she whispered. 'I . . .'

The sudden bite of his hand made her wince.

'You will do as I say, Elena,' he said sharply. 'Remember our deal.'

'I don't care about our deal,' she said desperately. 'I just don't want anything to happen to you. I . . .'

His sudden, passionate kiss silenced her. His hand clasped the back of her head, closing tightly on a handful of silky hair as his lips took hers. When he raised his head, his eyes were dark.

'I'll be back,' he whispered.

'Blake, don't . . .'

'*Hasta luego*, Princess.'

He was out of the truck before she could answer. Her heart pounded as she sat on the edge of the seat, watching as he moved up the road slowly and carefully, pausing now and then to sniff the air like a jaguar stalking its prey. Suddenly, he stepped to the side of the road and clambered up the slope. Elena held her breath as he stopped mid-way to the top and looked towards the rocky walls that rose on either side of the downed tree. Slowly, her pent-up breath began to hiss from between her open lips. Everything was fine; the forest was still silent. She smiled and put her hand on the door—when a piercing cry rent the air.

Men leaped out from behind boulders and trees at the top of the ravine. Elena shrank back in her seat. 'Run,' she whispered. Almost as if he'd heard the plea, Blake began to scramble down the slope. But it was useless. The men were on him like wolves on a deer, and they dragged him to the ground.

'No,' she whimpered, putting her hand to her mouth, 'no, please!'

Elena wrenched the door open and stumbled out of the truck. Quickly, she began to run back along the road. How long would it take her to get to Mazatal? They'd driven for two hours, maybe more. Dear God, it would take her many times that to get back. Her breath puffed in and out of her lungs. Six hours, maybe. Or eight. And then it would be another hour until she found the *policia* and told them her story, and then two or three hours again until the *policia* reached the spot where Blake had been taken by the bandits...

And that would be too late. Besides, if the *policia* recognised her as Eduardo Esteban's daughter, who knew what might happen? Blake needed help, and he needed it now.

Elena's footsteps slowed, then stopped. Above the rasp of her own breath, she heard the sounds of the forest. No one had seen her, she thought gratefully. At least she had that on her side. Quickly, she trotted off the road into the trees. Then, moving stealthily, she began to climb.

By the time she neared the abandoned truck, she could hear the bandits laughing and talking among themselves. Carefully, from behind leafy cover, she watched. Blake's hands had been bound behind his back, but he was on his feet. *Thank God,* Elena thought as she stared at him. His face was pale, and there was a thin smear of blood beside his mouth, but at least he was alive.

Her heart skipped a beat as one of the bandits hauled the carryall from the truck. What if he zipped it open and found her things, a woman's things? They might begin to search for her. But the carryall was passed from hand to hand and finally the last man draped it over his arm. Suddenly, there was a yell of triumph. A bandit had been poking beneath the seats, and now he held up a bottle of *tequila*. They'd found Manuel's private hoard, Elena thought. She watched as he opened it and took a long swallow. The man beside him laughed and snatched the bottle from him, drank, and then passed it on. Before long, the bottle was empty.

The bandits' laughter grew louder. One of them stuck a gun in Blake's ribs and Elena almost cried out, but Blake stood motionless and finally the man grinned and tucked the pistol into his pocket.

'Vamos,' he said, shoving Blake hard. One man climbed into the truck, started it, and drove it into a hidden clearing just off the road. He opened the hood and, to the sound of much laughter from his companions, he removed the rotor before joining them as they moved out, single file, along the road.

Hidden in the trees, Elena followed, wincing at what seemed like the loud crunching of her footsteps on the forest floor. But the bandits were noisy; they grew noisier after a second bottle of *tequila* had been opened and passed from man to man, and by the time they finally reached a trail that led off the road to their rude camp in the forest, she was no longer afraid they'd realise she was following them. They were drunk, laughing at Blake, taunting him with insults. All she feared now was that their alcohol-induced humour would become nasty before she could figure out a way to free him from the bandits' clutches.

But there was no reason to worry. The men drank through the morning and into the afternoon, trying to finish Manuel's private stock in one sitting. They had tied Blake to a tree on the far side of the camp; every now and then, one would stagger to his feet and shuffle off to relieve himself, invariably pausing beside Blake long enough to deliver an insult or threaten him with a pistol or a fist. But by the time the shadows began to lengthen, all but one of the bandits lay sprawled in a drunken stupor. Elena smiled grimly as the man yawned mightily, pushed his hat over his eyes, and leaned back against a tree. Within seconds, he, too, was snoring.

When she crept from the trees, Blake was so intent on trying to free his hands that she was almost upon him when he froze and then slowly lifted his head. His eyes widened in disbelief.

'Princess!'

The whispered word was an explosion. Her pulse raced as one of the men mumbled in his sleep, and she shook her head wildly. Freeing Blake from the ropes that bound him was difficult; it was as if the knots securing him were determined to defy her fingers. But finally he rose silently to his feet, grimacing as the blood flooded back to his limbs. Together, they untied his wrists; then, carefully, he retrieved the carryall which had been discarded in favour of Manuel's *tequila*.

'Hurry,' Elena pleaded in a silent whisper, and he nodded.

The two of them faded into the trees and then broke into a trot. They ran for what seemed like forever. When they were almost at the road, Elena's legs buckled. Blake caught her just as she began to slip to the ground.

'Can you go a little further, Princess?' he asked in an urgent whisper.

'Ju...just give me a minute to get my br...breath...'

His arm encircled her waist. 'Lean against me,' he said, drawing her against his side. 'That's my girl.' He watched her anxiously as she drew several deep breaths. 'OK now?' She nodded and they began walking, his arm still around her. 'I'd like to put a little more distance between those guys and us.'

Elena nodded. 'I thought ... I was afraid...'

She was still gasping for breath, and Blake drew her more closely against him. 'Don't worry, Princess. We'll be fine. They may have disabled the truck, but Manuel told me about a cave up here.' She looked at him, disbelief etched into her face. 'Yeah, I know, it's a long shot, but it's all we've got. He told me that when he and his cousin were *contrabandistas*, they used to hide out in a cave that's not far from where we are now.'

'But the bandits...'

He shook his head. 'They won't realise I'm gone for hours, Princess. That *tequila* is powerful stuff. And I don't think they'll come after me. It's not worth the effort. I mean, they got my wallet and the truck, and that's all they wanted.'

'Did they get our papers, too?' Elena drew air deep into her lungs. 'We're going to be in real trouble if...'

He laughed softly. 'Hell, they didn't even get our money.'

She glanced up at him. 'But you said...'

'I've been in enough places like this to know better than to make it easy for scum like them. They got a handful of *quetzals*, that's all. The rest, and our papers, are all tucked away safely in my belt.'

'Poor Manuel,' Elena whispered. 'His truck...'

'We'll buy him a new one, Princess. Don't worry about it. Just lean on me and keep moving. It's going to be dark soon, and I'd sure as hell like to be in that cave by then.'

She nodded. She hadn't the energy to tell him they'd never find the cave in these endless acres of forest. And that was just as well, because not long after that, Blake drew her into a rocky cleft in the hillside, dark and smelling faintly of animals, but still the most welcome sight imaginable.

Elena sank to the cave's leaf-strewn floor and leaned back against the rocky wall, watching while Blake built a fire. 'Bless you, Manuel,' she sighed. 'We're going to buy you the biggest, most beautiful truck in the world when this is over.'

Blake laughed. 'If we pack it full of *tequila*, he'll love it.' She nodded, eyes closed, listening to the crackling of the fire. 'Here,' he said. 'Take a drink of this.'

She opened her eyes. He was squatting beside her, holding out a flask. Elena took it from him and tilted it to her mouth. Water, tepid and slightly alkaline, trickled down her throat.

'Mmmm,' she said, wiping her chin with the back of her hand, 'delicious. Was that Evian or Perrier?'

'It was just water. And you ought to be damned glad we have it.'

Elena looked at him in surprise. His voice had gone flat and the expression on his face was grim.

'What's the matter?' she asked slowly.

He closed the flask and stuck it into the carryall. 'Come on, Princess. Don't play dumb. You know damned well.'

'No, I don't know. Are you worried about the bandits? You said...'

She gasped as Blake grasped her shoulders. 'What the hell do you mean by defying my orders?' he growled.

'Defying...' She stared at him.

'I told you you were to get the hell out if there was trouble. I told you not to look back. I...'

'Is this your idea of a joke? Because if it is...'

'Do I look as if I'm joking?'

Her eyes searched his face. 'No,' she said after a pause. 'No, you don't.'

'Damned right,' he said as he glared at her.

'But...'

'Never mind the excuses,' he snapped. 'Why the hell didn't you do as you were told?'

'You're impossible, do you know that?' she hissed. 'If I'd done as I'd been told, you'd still be sitting in that camp, listening to those *banditos* snore.'

'And you'd be in Mazatal.'

Elena's chin lifted. 'Exactly. And who knows what would have happened by the time I finally got somebody to come looking for you—*if* I got somebody, hmm?'

Firelight glinted in his dark eyes. 'Ah,' he said softly, 'now I understand. If something had happened to me, you'd have lost your safe conduct to Miami.'

Her voice quivered with anger. 'You really are a bastard, Blake Rogan,' she said. 'Do you really believe I'd...I'd risk my neck just because...just for...' Her voice broke and she turned her face away. 'If that's what you think...'

His hands spread along her shoulders and up her neck. 'No,' he said quietly, 'that's not what I think.' His fingers tangled in her dark hair and he moved closer to her. 'Look at me, Elena.'

The softness in his voice was mesmerising. Slowly, she turned and looked at him from beneath her lashes.

'Then...then why did you say it?' she whispered.

Blake tilted her head up and smiled. 'Maybe I just wanted to hear the reason from you.'

His eyes were dark, so dark. And they were asking for answers she didn't have. Elena swallowed drily.

'It...it just seemed like the right thing to do,' she murmured.

He smiled again. 'Did it?'

She could feel her heart racing. His hands were still in her hair, but now his fingers were caressing her, drawing lazy circles on the nape of her neck.

'Yes,' she whispered, 'I...I...'

'It was a dangerous thing to do,' he said softly. Her lashes fluttered as he leaned towards her and kissed the corner of her mouth. 'They might have seen you, Princess.' His arms closed around her and he eased her slowly down to the floor of the cave. The leaves were soft beneath her, and Blake's breath was warm upon her face.

'I . . . I didn't think about it,' she said, watching as the firelight danced across his face, touching his eyes with flecks of gold. 'But . . .'

Her eyelids fluttered closed as he brushed his lips across hers. 'I told you not to disobey me, Elena.' His mouth touched hers again, softly coaxing her lips apart.

His words were both a threat and a caress, and she shivered as his hand cupped her chin and he ran his thumb across the soft fullness of her lower lip.

'I didn't. I . . . I . . .' Her whispered words became a moan as his hand slid beneath her blouse. 'Blake,' she said in a broken whisper, 'please . . .'

'You made me a promise, Elena,' he murmured. His hand cupped her breast as his lips burned the soft skin in the hollow of her throat, and her pulse leaped in response, beating wildly against the excitement of his touch. 'Have you forgotten?'

Her eyes opened as he lifted his head. In the flickering glow of the fire, Blake's face was a shadowed mystery.

'No,' she said thickly. 'I was to be your . . . your dutiful wife.'

He bent to her and his mouth covered hers in a kiss that stole her breath away. 'And now, beautiful Princess, that's exactly what you will be.'

CHAPTER TEN

THE sharp taste of fear flooded her mouth. 'No!' she said, the word like the crack of a whip in the still air. In one lithe motion, Elena twisted her head away from him and stumbled to her feet. But Blake was on her in an instant, one hand tangling in her hair, the other clasping her waist, and his powerful body pinned her against the rocky wall of the cave.

'Don't fight me,' he whispered.

His mouth fell on hers like a hawk on its prey, taking her breath in a hard, demanding kiss. Elena whimpered and tried to pull free, but the hand threaded in her hair held her fast beneath his plundering mouth. Her heart was racing as if all the devils of hell were at her heels. When he finally lifted his head and looked into her eyes, she drew a shuddering breath.

'Don't do this,' she whispered. 'Blake, I beg you . . .'

His eyes burned into hers. 'Yes, go on, beg me.' His hand slid around her throat, the thumb lying in the pulsing hollow. 'Beg me, Elena,' he taunted, and he caught her mouth again in another long kiss that left her whimpering. 'You knew this had to happen,' he said in a voice so thick she barely recognised it.

Something wild and hot flamed to life deep within her. He was going to teach her a lesson, she thought, remembering those other times he'd kissed her into submission. Her bones felt as if they were melting, and she sagged against him.

'You're crazy,' she said in a choked whisper.

A strange smile flickered across his face. 'Yes, I must be. I should have done this days ago.'

'Blake,' she said, 'Blake, please...'

'Please, what?' he murmured.

He bent to her and his teeth closed lightly on her bottom lip. She moaned against his mouth.

'Blake,' she said again, 'listen to me. I...I know what you're doing...'

He laughed softly. 'Clever girl,' he said, touching his mouth to her throat.

'You're...you want to remind me that you're in charge...' She closed her eyes as he nuzzled the hollow of her throat. 'This...this business of trying to make me feel...feel vulnerable...'

Blake's arms slid beneath her, gathering her to him. 'Is that how you feel when I kiss you, Elena?'

Her heart thudded. 'No. Yes.' She drew in her breath as his tongue traced the line between her lips. 'Don't...don't do that,' she whispered. 'Blake, you have no right...'

His arms tightened around her. 'I have every right.' His hand clasped the back of her head and she gasped as he forced her face towards his. 'You're my wife.' His eyes burned into hers. 'That gives me the right. You belong to me. You've always belonged to me.'

The same wild heat licked through her again.

'You can't,' she said. 'Our marriage isn't real.'

'Isn't it?'

His mouth took hers again, his lips slanting down hungrily, imprisoning hers in a kiss that left her faint. When he lifted his head and looked down at her, his eyes were pools of darkness that she knew she could drown in. Elena drew a shuddering breath and then another before she had the strength to speak.

'You know it isn't. When we get to Miami...'

His mouth hardened into a narrow line. 'I know what happens when we get to Miami, Elena.' His hand moved over her. 'But tonight—tonight, we're in San Felipe.'

Her heart was racing so rapidly that it felt as if it were going to burst. But not with fear, she thought suddenly. No, it was something else that drove through her now, something that was already beginning to make her bones feel as if they had no substance.

'You...you're just trying to remind me that...that I have to do as you say.' She moaned as his hand moved across her, brushing lightly over her breast and down to her hip. 'And that...that you're a man and I'm a woman...'

'Hell, Princess, we both knew that the second we laid eyes on each other.'

His voice was husky; he exuded a maleness that made her breath quicken. She looked up at him, her eyes skittering across his face, touching on his flared nostrils, lingering on the midnight darkness of his eyes. How easily he could overpower her and take her, she thought suddenly. She'd have no choice but to let him do what he wished to her. There would be no way to stop him—and then it wouldn't be her fault and she'd never have to admit how badly she wanted him, not even to herself.

Her lashes fell to her cheeks. Dear God, this was madness! Was the fantasy of being taken against her will easier to face than reality? Yes, she thought, yes, it was, because the reality was that she *did* want him, she'd wanted him from the start. And the shame of that wanting, the pain of it, was more than she could bear. How could she want a man who'd been bought for her, a man she'd never see again after they reached the States?

'Elena?'

Blake's voice was like raw honey. Her eyes opened slowly and focused on him, on that hard mouth that had kissed her with such tenderness, on eyes that could be as cold as the sea or as deep as midnight, and her breathing quickened. He whispered her name again.

'Blake, please...'

'Put your arms around me,' he said huskily.

'No.' But, even as she whispered the word, her arms reached up to him. 'Tomorrow...'

His eyes darkened. 'The hell with tomorrow,' he said fiercely. 'This is now.'

His mouth came down on hers, searing her with heat. Elena whimpered as they sank to the ground together. Blake's hand was spread against her ribs, the pressure of his fingers seeming to penetrate her skin. His lips moved against hers, urging her mouth to open to him. The taste of his kiss made her tremble; when his tongue found hers, Elena shuddered and wound her arms around his neck, revelling in the hard strength of his body against hers.

'Elena, sweet Elena,' he whispered. She gasped as his fingers blazed a fiery path over her breasts and down her ribs, lingering on the curve of her belly, then moving to stroke her thighs. As if from a distance, she heard herself whisper his name, and the sound was caught in his kiss, returned to her on the moist warmth of his breath. Her mouth clung to his as her body stirred to life beneath his caresses.

Blake drew back and looked at her. 'My Princess,' he whispered, 'my beautiful Elena.'

In the smoky light of the fire, his features were a mask, highlighted by glints of amber and gold. Their eyes met and held; time stopped in that breathless moment. And then Blake gathered her to him again and captured her mouth in a long, slow kiss. Elena moaned as his tongue moved like a flame along the curve of her mouth.

'Your mouth is like nectar,' he murmured, his breath fanning her face with warmth. 'And your body—God, your body...'

She felt as if she were drowning in a velvet sea of sensation. His whispers, his caresses, the feel of him in her arms—Elena knew suddenly that she had waited a lifetime for this night. She sighed his name, and then her fingers tangled in the thick, silky hair at the back of his head and she drew him to her.

'Elena...' His hand slid down her throat, pausing at the pulse beating rapidly in the shadowed hollow, then moved gently to the swell of her breast. 'Tell me you want me to touch you,' he said raggedly. 'Tell me.'

Her answer was as quick and fierce as his kisses. 'Yes,' she said, 'yes, touch me.'

He groaned as his mouth swooped to hers, taking it with a ferocity that set her blood blazing. His hand cupped her breast, and she felt her nipple leap to meet his questing palm.

'Like this?'

Her eyes closed. 'That feels,' she whispered, 'it feels...'

'Yes,' he said, 'yes, sweet Elena.' He caught her bottom lip between his teeth and bit down gently. 'Now, you,' he whispered, bringing her hand to his chest.

Her fingers slid into the open neck of his shirt; his head fell back as her hand moved across his heated skin, and he murmured her name. She watched the pleasure on his face, lost in wonder that her touch could do to him what his did to her. His eyes closed and his lashes lay dark against his golden skin; his mouth narrowed as if the feathering stroke of her hand brought him pain. And then, suddenly, he reached for her and drew her to him fiercely, wrapping her in his arms as he kissed her.

There was a question in his kiss, and his lips on hers searched for the answer. Her hands moved up his chest, to his shoulders, and suddenly the answer was in her heart. Blake, she thought with shattering clarity, Blake, I love you . . .

His mouth sought hers again, this time demanding response, and she looked at him, letting him read her surrender in her eyes.

His hands were on the buttons of her shirt, and she stirred languidly as he parted the soft fabric and eased it from her shoulders. The fire was warm on her skin, its smoky fragrance mingling with the fresh scent of rain from the forest. But nothing was as warm as the feel of Blake's hands, nothing was as intoxicating as the smell of him as he gathered her into his arms.

His mouth descended on hers, hard, hungry and filled with need. She clung to him in a sudden flood of desire. Then, fingers trembling, she fumbled at the buttons of his shirt and drew it back from his chest.

'I want to feel you against me,' she said in a whisper. 'Is that all right?'

'Jesus,' he groaned, and he brought her up to him, his arms binding her to his body.

The feel of his skin against hers made her gasp with pleasure. There was a dark, fine mat of hair on his chest; the sensation of it against her breasts sent a tremor through her.

'Blake,' she sighed, 'Blake . . .'

There was so much more to tell him, but his name was all she could manage. And it seemed enough; his kisses moved from her lips to her eyelids to her hair as his hands moved on her skin, caressing, touching, learning her secrets.

She gasped as his hand cupped her naked breast, capturing its soft, swollen curve against the heat of his palm. His thumb moved across the nipple; she cried out again and turned towards him, seeking his kiss, her fingers curling into the thick hair at the nape of his neck.

She sank back in his arms as he whispered to her, as he touched her, as he caressed her with growing abandon. Her clothes fell away from her as if by magic; she felt the heat of the fire flicker over her naked flesh. Somewhere in the distance there was the sound of rain, but it was all part of a dream. The only reality was Blake's lovemaking.

'My Princess,' he murmured as he trailed his hand along her skin, the heat of his fingers igniting her until she moaned beneath his touch and moved blindly against his hand. Still, when his fingers cupped the dark triangle of her innocence, she caught his hand and held it, trepidation in her eyes.

'Blake?' Her voice was a silken whisper, question and answer all at once.

'Don't be afraid of me, Princess,' he whispered, and then he bent to her and his lips found her breast.

She called out his name as the moist heat of his mouth surrounded her swollen flesh. Her body quickened beneath his teeth and tongue, smoky waves of desire spreading through her, radiating from her breast to her loins. She cried out again and Blake drew her into his embrace, kissing her with a ferocity that left her trembling. Fireglow danced on his skin as he rose to his knees and stripped off his shirt.

'Elena,' he whispered, and she sighed and reached out to him, touching him as she had longed to touch him that night in the Indian village, trailing her hand down the narrowing dark line of hair that bisected his chest. He brought her hand to his lips, kissing the soft underside of her wrist. Then he stood, his eyes on hers as he unzipped his jeans and eased them down his hips. Her mind jumped to Margarita's sour warnings, to her schoolmates' furtive whispers. But there was no time to think or to wonder; Blake was beside her again, kissing her, touching her, and she was caught up in the fever of their passion.

'Elena,' he said thickly, *'mi amante...'*

Her head fell back as his hands moved slowly over her, lingering on her breasts, on the slight rounding of her belly, and when his fingers tangled in the silken dampness between her thighs, she clasped his hand and held it against her, trembling beneath the power of that gentle touch.

'Yes,' he whispered, and then his mouth followed the path his hands had left, his kisses hot against her flesh. And when finally his lips found the hidden delta that was the very centre of her, Elena cried out and arched against him in need.

'Now,' he said, and he moved against her, 'now, sweet Princess.'

She whispered his name as he cupped her buttocks and lifted her to him. Her muscles tensed at the sudden invasion and he held back, waiting while her body closed around him. Then, ready for a release she barely understood, Elena trembled in Blake's arms.

'Please,' she whispered.

A smile of triumph flashed across his face. 'Yes,' he said fiercely, 'yes.'

And just before the world fell away from her, just before Blake took her to the summit of a sunlit mountain and the fleeting moment of immortality that awaited her there, she thought of Margarita and the girls who had whispered in the night, and she sorrowed for them all.

Elena's eyes opened slowly as a searching finger of sunlight pierced the cave's gloom. A quick glance told her she was alone in the cave, and she stretched languorously, smiling a little as she remembered the night. Blake had made love to her again and again, each time more wonderful than the last. And then, finally, he'd curved his arm around her and brought her head to his chest.

'Sleep for a while, Princess,' he'd whispered. 'It's almost tomorrow.'

The words had knifed into her heart. Tomorrow, she'd thought, tomorrow... and then her lashes had fluttered to her cheeks and she'd fallen into a dreamless sleep.

It was morning now—all too soon, tomorrow had arrived. No, she thought, no, not yet. There would be another tomorrow, at least—they were still miles from the border. That meant there was time...

'Good morning.'

She looked up, startled by the sound of Blake's voice. He was standing in the entrance to the cave, and she had the sudden feeling he'd been watching her for long minutes.

'Good morning,' she said. She waited, a faint smile trembling on her lips. Surely there was more to say than that. But Blake said nothing. His eyes were in shadow, unreadable, although she could see his mouth, a thin, hard line against the stubble of his beard. Suddenly, her throat felt like sandpaper. 'Has it...has the rain stopped?' she asked.

'Yes. A couple of hours ago. It looks as if it's going to be hot as hell later on.'

Again she waited, and then, at last, she cleared her throat. 'Well, then, I guess I'll—er—I'll get dr...'

She couldn't say the word. God, that was stupid, wasn't it? She'd lain naked in Blake's arms all night and now she stumbled over telling him she was going to get dressed. She swallowed and looked away from him. No, it wasn't stupid, she thought. Her nudity hadn't embarrassed her while he'd made love to her. Now, somehow, it did.

Blake nodded. 'Yes,' he said, his eyes flickering over her body, 'that's a good idea.'

Elena fought against the desire to curl into a tight ball. 'Right,' she said quickly. 'Maybe you could...you could start a fire so we can have some coffee after I...before we leave.'

He nodded. 'I'll be back in a minute.'

Her hands trembled as she reached for her clothing and dressed. It wasn't as if she'd expected a miracle. Yes, there had been one heart-stopping moment in the darkest hour of the night when she'd stirred beneath Blake and let herself dream of hearing him say he loved her. But it was daylight, and the time for dreams was past. All she wanted now was for him to say something tender. Please, she thought, let him smile at me or kiss me or...

'That should do it.'

He was back, carrying an armload of firewood. Elena watched as he dropped it to the ground, and then she reached for the carryall.

'I'll—um—I'll get out the coffee. And the sugar. And...'

She knew she was babbling, but she couldn't stop until Blake began walking towards her. Her heart began to race. He was going to take her into his arms; he was going to kiss her. He was going to smile at her and say...

'I'm glad you're awake. I ran out of cheroots hours ago.' Her brows drew together as he took the carryall from her. 'I've been dying for a smoke. But my last pack of the damned things is in here and I didn't want to disturb you.'

She watched in silence as he dug out the cheroots and then lit up. Smoke drifted lazily towards the roof of the cave and she inhaled shakily. The musky smell of tobacco would always remind her of Blake, she thought suddenly, and of this moment, this terrible moment...

'Blake.'

She spoke in a low voice, the single word rushing from her lips before she could call it back. He looked up at her from where he squatted beside the fire he'd started, his eyes narrowed against the smoke.

'Blake,' she said again, 'what's the matter? We...we're behaving as if we...as if we were strangers.'

His teeth bit down on the cheroot. 'I don't know what you mean.'

'Yes, you do. You...'

'Hand over the flask, will you? And the pot.' She hesitated and then did as he'd asked. 'Thanks.'

'You see? You're so polite, so civil...'

His eyebrows rose as he filled the little pot and set it over the fire. 'Would you prefer it if I weren't?'

There was a sudden tightness in her throat. 'Blake?' Her voice was a throaty whisper. 'Please, tell me what's wrong.'

He rose slowly to his feet. 'You know what's wrong,' he said after a moment. His eyes met hers and then slid away. 'Last night never should have happened.'

Her heart tumbled crazily, 'But it did. It...'

'It was a mistake.'

It seemed to take enormous effort to speak. 'You didn't think so last night,' she said carefully.

Blake raked his fingers through his hair. 'Hell, last night I didn't think at all.'

Pale colour washed her cheeks and she took a step towards him. 'I just meant...I thought...'

His eyes blazed into hers. 'It's too damned bad you didn't think last night.'

His words, sharp as a razor, sliced into her heart. 'I see,' she said slowly, her eyes locked with his, 'that's how it works. When it suits you, you tell me not to think. And when it doesn't, you tell me...'

His head lifted. 'All I'm telling you is that what we did—what happened was a mistake.' He raked his fingers through his hair and took a deep breath. 'Look, I'm trying to apologise. I guess I'm making a mess of it, but...'

Her eyes fixed on his face. He was still talking, but she'd given up listening. Why would he apologise for making love to her? He'd seduced her, yes, but God knew she'd been willing. Most women probably were, she thought, looking at his hard, handsome face and body. For a moment, she felt a stab of sympathy for the faceless women in his past. Had some been foolish enough to think a night of lovemaking meant a life of love? Had some believed the morning would bring a commitment with it?

There was a painful tightness in her throat. Rogan wasn't a man for commitment. He'd take what he wanted from a woman, but he'd never belong to her, not unless she laid a trap he couldn't evade and tricked him into marriage...

Oh, God! The realisation was as dizzying as a ride on a roller coaster. *The annulment.*

That's what this was all about. Rogan wasn't sorry—he was panicked. Annulments became difficult, perhaps impossible, if a marriage had been consummated. And divorce could be a lengthy, involved procedure if one party chose to make it so. It would take a lawyer an hour to define the technicalities, but it took only a minute to define Rogan's concerns. He was afraid he was trapped, and he was scurrying to get away, like a bug running from a rolled-up newspaper.

Elena closed her eyes. He was just what she'd thought he was. An adventurer, an opportunist—the pain she'd felt a short while before changed to rage. It was a safer emotion to face, and she welcomed it. She wanted to slap his face, to scar him. And she would, she thought, watching him through narrowed eyes. But there was a better way to hurt a man like Rogan.

'You're right,' she said, her voice cutting across his. 'It was a mistake. I'm glad you know it, too.'

His mouth curved downward. 'Yes, that's what I thought. I...'

Elena lifted her chin. 'You took advantage of me, Rogan.'

Rogan blew out a breath. 'I'm sorry, Elena. I...'

Now, she told herself, now, while you still can... 'Don't be sorry. Now, we both have something to remember.'

He took a step towards her. 'Elena, listen to me...'

'You got a bonus for the job my father paid you to do. And I...'

She flinched as his hands closed on her shoulders. 'It wasn't like that,' he growled. 'What kind of man do you think I am?'

It took all her determination to look into his eyes without breaking. 'The kind I thought you were from day one,' she whispered. 'My father and I both paid more than your services were worth.'

Blake's eyes darkened, then turned to winter ice. She waited, listening to the heavy rasp of his breath, certain she'd pushed him too far. And just when she thought she'd cry out from the bite of his fingers on her flesh, his hands fell to his sides.

'You really are your father's daughter, *señorita*,' he growled.

'That's right,' she said sharply, 'I am. I'm an Esteban, and proud of it.'

He looked at her, an unreadable expression on his face. Then he let out his breath in a weary sigh.

'The highway's just below us,' he said. 'I scouted the mountain while you were asleep. We covered more ground than I realised yesterday.'

It was over. 'And the border? Is it near?'

'Probably less than an hour.' Rogan moved away and kicked dirt on to the smouldering fire. 'We'll be in Miami tonight.'

He turned and looked at her, his eyes cold and empty. Elena was the first to turn away.

'I can't think of anything I want more,' she said.

But it was a lie. There were lots of things she wanted more. Not to have met Blake Rogan, for one. Not to have fallen in love with him, for another. And most of all, she thought as she followed him down the mountain, most of all, she wished she didn't still love him.

But she did.

CHAPTER ELEVEN

FLORIDIANS hate to admit that Miami's weather is ever less then perfect. Most of the time, the days are warm and the nights pleasant. But once in a while, when summer grips the city, there are days so hot and humid that the air seems to have the consistency of a suffocating blanket. It's Nature's reminder to everyone that the gleaming city beside the sea stands on land that was once swamp. On such days, the white beaches are crowded but the streets are empty. And so are the shops.

On a day of blazing August heat, the Fisher Art Gallery was as deserted as any of the stores surrounding it. The gallery was located in a shopping mall in Miami Beach, which is not a beach at all but an island community just across Biscayne Bay from the city of Miami on the mainland. Usually, tourists as well as locals were drawn into the elegant little gallery by its distinctive window displays. But on this hot August afternoon, with the temperature and the humidity both over ninety degrees Fahrenheit, the gallery hadn't had a single customer. Not a real one, Elena thought as the door swung open and yet another sweating tourist stumbled in.

The man's camera swung from his neck as he shook his head in response to her polite offer of assistance.

'Just looking,' he gasped, while his wife drew in lungfuls of artificially chilled air.

Elena nodded. 'Of course,' she said pleasantly. 'Call me if you have any questions.'

Jeremy Fisher's eyebrows rose as she moved past him to the back of the shop. She shook her head discreetly and busied herself with a box of deKooning posters that had arrived that morning. After a few minutes, the bell above the door tinkled again and Elena looked up.

'I'm beginning to feel like the local Red Cross,' she said with a smile. 'Those poor souls looked as if they were going to collapse.'

'Well, the next case of heat prostration is going to have to find another hole to crawl into,' her employer said. 'Leave those posters until tomorrow, Elena. I'll set the alarm and we'll call it a day.'

Elena looked at the art deco clock above the door. 'But it's hours till closing time, Jeremy.'

'The only thing we could sell today is ice-cream,' he said, smiling at her. 'Besides, there are better things to do in this heat.'

'Sure there are,' she laughed. 'You can tuck yourself into a tub full of ice or curl up in the refrigerator or...'

'Or drive down to Plantation Key for dinner. Remember that little place on the water, the one where we had those terrific crabcakes? We can be there before you know it.'

Elena smiled and shook her head. 'Sorry. I have a million things to do tonight, Jeremy. I...'

Her boss sighed. 'Yeah, I know. You have to wash your hair. Or write a letter to your father. Or read a book. Or...'

'Jeremy, please, don't make it sound like that. I...'

'Do you know how many times we've gone out in the past four months?' he asked as he rested his hands lightly on her shoulders.

'I can't help it if I'm busy,' Elena said quickly. 'I...'

'Three,' he said, 'and only because I badgered you.' His fingers spread on her shoulders, gently kneading her knotted muscles. 'I wish you'd tell me what's troubling you, Elena. You haven't been yourself since you returned from San Felipe.'

'Nothing's troubling me. I've told you that. I...'

Jeremy shook his head. 'There are shadows beneath your eyes, you've lost weight...'

Elena forced a smile to her face. 'That's it,' she said, 'spoil me with compliments.'

'Elena, dear...'

'There are things on my mind, that's all. My father...'

Jeremy shook his head. 'Your father's fine. The revolution is over, things are back to normal.'

'Almost back to normal. There are still problems.'

'Elena.' Jeremy's fingers pressed into her shoulders. 'You'll never get on with your life until you're free of that man.'

'What's that supposed to mean?' she asked sharply, pulling away from him.

Jeremy watched her for a moment. 'I only meant that he hasn't signed the annulment papers yet.' His warm brown eyes searched her face. 'That does bother you, doesn't it?'

'Yes, of course,' she said quickly, turning her back to him.

'What do your father's lawyers say now?'

Elena swung around to face him. 'What is this, Jeremy? A quiz?' The words were hardly out of her mouth before she held her hand out to him. 'Forgive me, please. I didn't mean to snap at you.'

Jeremy took both her hands in his. 'I only meant that perhaps there was something that stood in the way of the annulment.'

Colour bloomed in her cheeks. 'Don't be silly. Rogan and I were...our marriage was just a legal formality. I never...we never...'

'Hey!' Jeremy's voice was soft. 'All I meant was that maybe this guy was holding out for something. Maybe he wants more money before he signs.'

'Rogan got his money. My father...'

'Maybe he wants more,' her boss said gently. 'After all, the guy's not exactly Mr Clean. The man's a drifter.'

'Rogan's not a drifter,' Elena said. 'He travels a lot, yes, but...'

'Elena, come on! What kind of man marries a woman for money?'

Elena pulled her hands from his. 'Yes, but he could have left me behind a dozen times and he didn't. I told you that, Jeremy. I...' She paused and then laughed shakily. 'Look this is silly. He hasn't signed because the solicitors' office hasn't located him. It's that simple. He told them he'd be in Fiji but he wasn't. And...'

'Exactly. He's a drifter, just as I said. Dammit, I still don't understand how your father could have entrusted you to a man like that.'

'I told you what happened, Jeremy. There was no other way.'

'But a man like that...'

'"A man like that",' Elena said sharply, mimicking his critical tone, 'is the reason I didn't end up trapped in San Felipe.' She stared at him in silence and then turned away. 'Now, if you're all done with this interrogation, I'm going to get my bag and go home.'

Jeremy followed after her into the storeroom. 'Why is it we always end up arguing about Rogan? You defend him and...'

'Oh, for God's sake,' she said, spinning around to face him, 'I do not defend him. But you make these ridiculous accusations and...' Her words broke off and she sighed. 'All right. I'm sorry I bit your head off. You're right, of course. The papers should have been signed and returned long ago. I'll call the solicitors as soon as I get home. There must be something they can do to speed things up.'

Jeremy smiled. 'That's the ticket.' His arms closed around her. 'And then we can set our wedding date.'

Elena's eyebrows rose. 'Jeremy,' she said gently, 'I haven't said I'd marry you.'

His smile widened. 'A mere technicality, Miss Esteban; one I hoped you wouldn't notice.'

She laughed softly. 'What am I going to do with you, hmm?'

'Become my wife,' he said quickly. 'I'll make you happy, Elena. I promise.'

She closed her eyes as he brought her closer to him and kissed her. Marriage to Jeremy would be like his kisses, she thought as his lips pressed against hers. It would be pleasant, easy-going—and dull. It would be nothing like marriage to Blake. With Blake, each day would be an adventure. And each night, oh God, each night . . .

Elena put her hands against Jeremy's chest and stepped back. 'I'll see you tomorrow.'

He nodded. 'Try to get a good night's sleep, Elena. And remember . . .'

'Call the lawyers' office,' she said with a quick smile. 'I know.'

The receptionist who took her call was polite, as always. She promised to bring it to the immediate attention of one of the senior partners, also as always. Elena sighed as she hung up the phone. How many times had she made the same call in the past months?

She rose and kicked off her shoes. Her apartment was warm; perhaps it was crazy, but she preferred to turn off the air conditioning and throw open the windows, even on a day like this. Her windows overlooked the ocean, and she loved the smell and the sound of the sea as it beat against the shore. Quickly, she peeled off her dress and underthings and slipped into a long robe. Later, she'd shower and poke in the refrigerator for some dinner—a carton of yogurt or some fruit and cheese would do—but for now, all she wanted was to sit beside the window and stare at the aquamarine water.

Elena sighed wearily and sank into the chair. What was it Jeremy had said? That she'd never get on with her life until she was free of Blake Rogan. She put her head back and closed her eyes, letting her mind run free of the tight control she'd imposed upon it.

Jeremy didn't know how right he was. Blake was in her thoughts all the time, even when she least expected him to be. She dreamed about him every night, but she'd expected that. It was all the other times she thought about him that were wearing her down. Like yesterday, when she'd seen the dorsal fins of a school of dolphins cutting through the water, or last week, when a shooting star had arced across the midnight sky, or even this morning, when she'd cut her finger opening the box of deKooning posters...

When she was happy, she thought of Blake. And when she was sad, she thought of him, too. It was as if—as if she needed to share everything, the good and the bad, with him. And, God help her, it was getting worse, not better.

Elena shook her head. If only Blake had signed the damned annulment papers when he was supposed to. She knew he'd contacted her father's lawyers the day after they returned to Miami, just as she had. But then he'd vanished.

'What do you mean, you don't know where he is?' Elena had demanded. 'Didn't he leave an address?'

He had. A hotel on the Beach—one of the most luxurious and expensive ones, the solicitor had added with a curl of surprise in his unctuous voice. But he wasn't there any more.

'Well, what about a forwarding address?' Elena had asked.

This time, the lawyer's eyebrows had curled to match his voice. 'Fiji,' he'd said with a touch of disbelief.

'Just Fiji?'

'Just Fiji. Believe me, Señorita Esteban, we're doing what we can. We'll find him.'

Elena sighed as she rose from the chair and padded across the room to the kitchen alcove. They hadn't found him, she thought as she poured herself a glass of iced lemonade. Fiji had led to Tahiti and Tahiti had led to Singapore and Singapore had led nowhere. Blake's whereabouts were still a mystery, which meant the papers were unsigned. She was still his wife.

Blake's wife... Elena sank down in the chair beside the window again, remembering the last time anyone had referred to her that way. It was on the flight from Mexico City to Miami. The flight attendant had called her 'Mrs Rogan' each time she stopped by to flash her professional smile and ask if Elena was sure she hadn't changed her mind and decided she wanted something. But all Elena had wanted was what no one but Blake could give her, and so she kept flashing an equally polite smile and saying no, thank you very much, she didn't want anything to eat or drink or read or...

And all the while, Blake had sat beside her, silent and hard as a stone, which was the way he'd been since they'd left the cave in San Felipe. He'd spoken to her only a couple of times after that. The first was at the Mexican border when he'd warned her to smile and keep still. Elena had been sure they'd be stopped from crossing over: they were on foot and they looked like tramps. But Blake had put his arm around her and greeted the guards with a cheerful *'Buenos días, muchachos.'* Their surly faces had remained impassive as he'd held out their travel documents, but when they had seen the flash of green currency tucked within, they had muttered and motioned them on.

Vamanos, they had said abruptly, and just that quickly the dangers of revolution-torn San Felipe were behind them. They had walked for a while, then caught a ride on the back of a hay wagon to the airport at Tuxtla Gutierrez, where they'd bought the last seats on a flight to Mexico City. And once they'd reached Mexico City, they were practically home.

When they landed at Miami Airport, Elena blinked in the sudden glare of lights. It was really over now, she thought, glancing at Blake as he walked beside her. They would probably never see each other again. Her eyes moved over him slowly, as if to commit to memory the aggressive thrust of his jaw and the lithe movement of his body. Would he at least say goodbye? she wondered, hating him and loving him and telling herself that if she broke down and cried she'd never forgive herself.

But Rogan said nothing. He touched her arm—lightly, although she would always remember that the shock of his touch seemed to reverberate through her body—and led her to the taxi line. The terminal was uncrowded at that hour of the night; a cab was waiting and he led her to it.

This was it, then, she thought, this was how love would end. But it wasn't love, not for Blake. He'd taken what he wanted from her, and now he was moving on. He'd made that painfully clear. This was the moment of their parting, and it was for the best that it had come so quickly.

It's for the best... Elena Teresa Maria Consuelo Kelly-Esteban had been told that dozens of times. It was what was said to her each time someone she loved left her, and, each time, she'd swallowed her tears and accepted the pain of parting. Why couldn't she accept it now? Why did she feel as if her heart was made of glass, as if it were about to shatter?

And then, suddenly, Blake turned and grasped her shoulders. 'Elena,' he said, and then he muttered a savage oath and pulled her roughly into his arms, holding her so tightly that he almost stopped her breath. His head bent to hers, his eyes as dark as the pits of Hell.

'Goodbye, Princess,' he whispered, and then his mouth captured hers. Time stopped while he kissed her with a desperate hunger that, at the end, changed to a tenderness that made her weep, and she knew she would remember this bittersweet moment for the rest of her life. When finally he let her go, she was trembling.

'Blake,' she whispered.

But he was gone. And he had taken her heart and soul with him.

Elena jumped as the telephone's shrill cry pierced the silence. Jeremy, she thought, sighing a little. He meant well, but she didn't need a man to fuss over her. She needed a man to make her heart sing, one who could make her laugh and cry and...

But it wasn't Jeremy. It was the lawyer, returning her call. She sighed and settled back into the chair, her legs tucked beneath her, readying herself for this week's report. Heaven only knew where they'd have traced Blake to this time. Not that it mattered; he was always one step ahead of any attempt to intercept him.

Elena straightened in her seat. The voice purring into her ear was filled with uncommon good cheer.

'Good news, Miss Esteban. We located Mr Rogan.'

Suddenly, it seemed difficult to breathe. 'You . . . you found him?'

'Better still, he's returned the papers to us.'

Elena's heart stopped. 'Signed?' she whispered.

'Signed, notarised—all legal and proper. He mailed them from some God-forsaken place in Africa. Apparently, they've been a couple of weeks in transit. Well, never mind. They've arrived, that's all that matters. I knew you'd be eager to see them, so I've taken the liberty of sending the papers to you by messenger.' The deep voice exuded satisfaction. 'It's all over, Miss Esteban.'

'All over?' she repeated foolishly.

The man chuckled. 'Hard to believe after all this time, isn't it? Yes, you're a free woman. To all intents and purposes, the marriage between you and Blake Rogan never took place. If you'd stop in tomorrow morning, say at around ten o'clock, we can . . .'

The phone slipped from her hand. It was over. All over. She was free. Her hands began to shake and she looked at them blankly before clasping them together in her lap.

Her eyes lifted to the window, to the waves licking against the white sand. Blake, she thought, Blake . . . He had signed the papers. She rose slowly and drew her robe around her. Her skin felt clammy and cool, and she wondered for a moment if the weather had changed suddenly. But she knew it hadn't; the chill that enveloped her had nothing to do with the temperature.

She'd been expecting this day for weeks—and now it was here. The last tenuous link that bound her to Blake was broken. She was free. Free to start her life again, Jeremy would say. Free of Rogan, her father would say. Free of legal encumbrances, the attorney would say. And that was what she'd been waiting for, wasn't it? It was what she needed before she could exorcise Blake's ghost.

She could put the whole episode behind her, forget it ever happened...

Her head fell forward. Forget? Forget those days with Blake? Forget the night when he'd held her in his arms and taught her about love? No, she thought, no, not love, not for him. Never for him. She'd been a job he'd been paid to do. Tears filled her eyes. Surely there had been moments when there had been more to it than that, moments when he'd looked at her and held her and felt something? Oh, God, she wanted so desperately to believe that.

Stop being a fool, Elena. This wasn't one of those romances where the Prince and the Princess loved happily ever after. What was it he'd said his friends called him? Rogue, that was it, and that's what he was, a rogue who would never be tamed.

Her head lifted. The doorbell was ringing. The messenger with the annulment papers, she thought, opening the door slowly. Still, when she saw the boy standing there, holding out a large manila envelope, she felt as if her legs were going to give way.

'Miss? Aren't you going to take this?'

Elena nodded, but she didn't move. The boy was looking at her as if she were insane, and maybe she was. After all, the papers inside the envelope changed nothing; the annulment was just a formality. Her marriage to Blake had never been real. The whole thing had been a deal with the devil, and her mother had been wrong. It wasn't enough to face him without fear; when you dealt with the devil, you had to be prepared to pay his price.

Finally, she reached out and took the envelope. When she closed the door, she trembled as she leaned her back against it. Should she open the envelope? Yes, of course...no, no, what was the point? She knew what was in it. And as foolish as it was, she didn't want to see the scrawl of Blake's name, and the ease with which he'd signed away what had been between them.

You really are crazy! she told herself. There wasn't anything between you, you fool. There had been a night's madness, but that was all. That was everything.

'Open the envelope, Elena,' she said aloud. 'It's time you faced reality. Just do it and get on with your life...'

...if you ever can.

She started at the sound of the doorbell. What now? She wasn't expecting anyone—unless Jeremy had decided to try and coax her into changing her mind about dinner at Plantation Key. Elena moaned softly. She wasn't up to dealing with him tonight.

'Jeremy,' she said, pulling open the door, 'I know you mean well, but I'm really not in the moo...'

Her words tumbled into silence. Blake Rogan stood in the doorway, filling it with his presence, looking as he had the night of her birthday party a lifetime ago. He was handsome in a dark blue suit that fitted his leanly muscled body with custom-made precision. Beneath it, she could see a pale blue shirt and a striped silk tie. His hair was still a bit long, she thought as her bewildered gaze travelled slowly over him, and there was a half-smoked cheroot clamped between his teeth, but other than that he looked as urbane as she'd ever seen him.

He stared at her in silence and then his mouth curved in a lazy smile. 'Hello, Princess. It's been a long time.'

'Four months,' she said dazedly, 'two weeks, and...' She clamped her lips together as his smile broadened into a smirk. 'What are you doing here, Blake?'

He took the cheroot from between his teeth. 'I was hoping you might figure it out for yourself,' he said softly.

Her heart began a dizzying spiral. Please, please, let this be a miracle.

She said nothing and, after a moment, Blake scowled and tossed the cheroot aside.

'I've come for the papers,' he said.

Elena shook her head. 'The papers? I don't understand . . .'

'Come on, Princess,' he said brusquely, shouldering his way past her, 'don't play dumb. The annulment papers.' He put his hands on his hips and looked at her. 'The receptionist at the law office told me you had them.'

'Yes, I have them,' she said slowly, 'but . . .'

Rogan reached past her and slammed the apartment door shut.

'I want them,' he growled, and he took a step towards her. 'And I want them right now.'

CHAPTER TWELVE

ELENA'S hands shook as she drew her robe more closely around her. Yes, of course, she thought—the lawyer had said the papers had been lost in transit. Rogan had become impatient for their return and he'd come for them himself. That was why he was here—there was no other reason, even if her foolish heart wanted to believe there was.

'The annulment papers,' she repeated. 'I have them right here. Do they have to be filed or...'

His voice cut across hers. 'Give them to me.'

'Look, whatever has to be done will be done. I'm sorry if... They only reached me today, you see, and...'

Rogan glowered at her. 'Jesus, some things never change. I didn't ask you for a speech, Elena. I asked you to give me the damned papers.'

Her head lifted slowly. 'I wasn't making a speech, I was simply trying to explain that...'

'Did I ask you for an explanation?'

His eyes were dark, his mouth curved in that half-smile she remembered so well. No, she thought, nothing had changed. Beneath the elegant suit, he was still the same rogue he'd always been. But he couldn't intimidate her any more. Not here, not in her own home.

'Listen, Rogan, I think you...' Her cool determination faltered as he moved towards her. 'Stop this right now, Rogan. I...'

'You have one hell of a short memory, Princess,' he said softly. 'Have you forgotten our deal? You don't think, you don't explain, you don't do anything except

172

what I tell you to do.' His eyes swept over her, lingering on the rapid rise and fall of her breasts beneath the thin summer robe, and then returned to her face. 'Give me the papers.'

Elena took a deep breath. 'I will. But I won't permit you to intimidate me.' Her voice was steady, which amazed her, because her heart was racing like a rabbit fleeing the shadow of a hawk.

His lips drew back in a quick smile. 'Is that what I'm doing?'

He moved closer to her, so close that she could see herself reflected in the midnight darkness of his eyes. Her breath hissed between suddenly dry lips as she filled her lungs.

'Stop it, Rogan. We're not in San Felipe any more.'

He smiled again and reached out to her, and ran his hand gently along her cheek. She trembled at his touch; suddenly, his eyes turned black and his voice became a rough whisper.

'Where we are hasn't a damned thing to do with it, Princess.'

'I don't know what you're talking about. You just...' Her words drifted away into the warm air. There was no sense in lying. Of course she knew. She had spoken of intimidation, but he had spoken of desire, and it was useless to deny it. He knew what he was doing to her— he'd always known, from the beginning. Elena's eyes met his. 'Don't do this,' she said softly.

Rogan's hand slid into her hair. 'Don't do what?' he murmured.

'Don't...don't play with me.' Her tongue felt swollen, and it took effort to swallow. 'Let me just get you the papers.'

'Your lawyers must have spent a bloody fortune running me to earth, Princess.' He smiled at her. 'I guess old Jeremy was getting impatient, hmm?'

He took a last step towards her. They were so close now that, if she wanted to touch him, she had only to lift her hand. But she didn't. She stood there instead, trying not to breathe as Rogan's fingers tangled in her hair and brushed the nape of her neck.

'Would you . . . will you please stop that?' she said in a rush. 'I find it . . . it's . . . I can't concentrate when you . . . Rogan, dammit!'

He smiled as his hand curved around the back of her head. 'Speaking of Jeremy, where is he?' His gaze went to the open window. The sun was setting, and the ocean lay in blue-grey shadow. 'Doesn't he spend his nights with you, Princess?'

Elena drew her breath. She could fell the heat of his body, smell his familiar scent.

Stop it, Elena, she thought desperately. Don't let him do this to you. He's playing games, that's all. He's reminding you that he's still in command. But this isn't San Felipe. This is Miami, for heaven's sake. Get yourself together and tell him to let you alone. Just sound as if you mean what you say.

His arms slid around her before she could speak. 'Have you and Jeremy set the date yet?'

Elena shook her head. 'We . . . no, no we haven't,' she said, standing stiffly within the circle of his arms. 'We . . .' She drew in her breath sharply as he brushed his mouth against hers. 'Dammit, Rogan . . .'

'Why not, Princess? Is it because he knows about us?'

'Rogan . . .'

'Does he?'

'He . . . he knows we were married. Of course he knows that. I . . .'

His arms tightened around her. Despite herself, she was drawn against his hard body. Her hands came up between them, flattening against his chest. She could feel the race of his heart under her palms.

'Does he know that I made love to you, Elena?' he whispered. 'Does he know that you trembled in my arms all through that night?'

Heat flooded through her. 'Rogan, don't.'

Slowly, inexorably, he gathered her to him until nothing separated them but the warmth of his breath.

'Blake,' he said. 'We settled that in San Felipe, remember?' His lips brushed her hair, her forehead, her cheek, his kisses like the drift of a leaf on the wind. 'I'm your husband, Elena. Wives don't call their husbands by their last names.'

Tears, swift and unexpected, filled her eyes. 'Damn you, Rogan,' she whispered, 'don't do this. Please, I beg you.'

His laughter was soft and triumphant. 'You begged me that night, too, Princess. I've lived on that memory for months.'

Elena's face lifted to his. 'Why are you doing this to me, Blake?' she asked in a broken murmur. 'The annulment papers...'

'To hell with the annulment papers,' he said fiercely, and his mouth dropped to hers.

His kiss demanded everything from her; for the rush of a heartbeat, Elena held back. She'd already given him too much, she thought wildly. He had wanted her passion, but she'd given him her heart. And then, unexpectedly, the kiss softened, became indescribably tender, and she was lost.

She'd ached for his touch and thirsted for his kisses, and now he was here, in her arms. He was warm and real, and she would not send him away. There had been too many empty nights already; in the years ahead, there would be thousands more. She would not surrender this moment, this night with the man she loved.

She would remember it all, she told herself while her arms lifted to him. She would store away each caress against the lonely future. She would be Blake's wife, this one last time.

Her arms curled around his neck as he swept her into his arms. 'Elena, *mi amante*,' he whispered as he lowered her to the wide sofa that faced the window.

His lover. If only she were, if only she were his lover, his love...

'You're so beautiful, Elena.' She closed her eyes as he opened her robe and eased it from her shoulders. 'Look at me, Princess,' he said softly. 'Don't you want to see the way you make me feel when I touch you?'

Her lashes lifted and she trembled when she saw his face. It was tense with desire, dark with need. He reached out and touched his hand to her throat, then brought it slowly down her body, over her breasts, to her belly, to her thighs, and she moaned and moved against his fingers as they parted her and sought her moist warmth.

'Blake,' she gasped, 'Blake...'

She watched as he pulled off his jacket and tie, and then she reached out and helped him strip away the rest of his clothing, her fingers moving as quickly as his, until finally he was naked beside her.

'Kiss me, Princess,' he said, bending to her, and she put her hands along either side of his face and drew his mouth to hers, revelling in the sweet possession of his lips, sighing at the faint rasp of his skin against her skin.

'Touch me,' he whispered, and her hands glided over him, over the hard planes of his arms and chest, the ridged muscles in his abdomen, and when finally she touched the heated velvet maleness of him, Blake drew in his breath and groaned his pleasure.

'Elena,' he said, 'Elena, *mi corazon*.'

'Yes,' she sighed, 'yes, oh yes.' I love you, she thought, and her heart felt as if it would burst with the terrible need to say the words aloud, to tell him what she had longed to tell him for so many months.

'Blake,' she said, 'listen...'

'Don't you ever stop talking?' he asked in a fierce whisper.

He kissed her then, kissed her mouth, her breasts, all the shadowed places that had hungered for him for so long.

'My beautiful Princess,' he whispered. 'My wife.'

And then he gathered her to him and the world spun away.

When she awakened, it was late. The room was dark, the sky visible through the window was a black abyss with starfires blazing in its far depths. Elena could hear the pounding of the ocean, smell the salt tang of the sea. And she was alone.

She sat up quickly and switched on the light, blinking in the sudden glare. Her robe lay beside the bed where Blake had dropped it, and she reached for it and pulled it on. His clothing was gone—and so were the annulment papers.

'Oh, God!'

The cry burst from her throat, ripping the silent fabric of the night, and Elena buried her face in her hands. Blake was gone, and she'd never see him again. Her heart was empty—emptier than it had been before. How stupid she'd been to think she could store up memories against the future! She couldn't do that—nobody could. You could only hope that some day, the pain would ease;

that, some day, you could remember and smile instead of sorrow; that . . .

'What kind of town is this, anyway? There's not a store open.'

Elena's hands fell from her face. 'Blake?' she whispered.

He grinned at her from the doorway. 'It sure as hell had better be,' he said. 'If old Jeremy's got a key, he'll just have to hand it over.'

Her eyes swept over him, from his bare feet—*bare feet?*—to his tousled hair.

'Where . . . where were you?'

He closed the door behind him and dropped his jacket on the chair. 'On the beach,' he said, padding towards her. 'How do you manage to look so beautiful in the middle of the night?' he asked and kissed her.

'But . . . but your shoes . . .'

'Under the couch,' he said with a wicked smile. 'Or the chair. Or—who the hell knows? I didn't want to put on the light and wake you.' He sat down beside her and slipped his arm around her. 'But I'm glad you're up. Maybe you can tell me where a guy can buy a bottle of champagne around here.'

Elena shook her head. 'At this hour?' She shook her head again. 'Blake, maybe I'm still half asleep. I don't underst . . .'

He kissed her again, a longer, deeper kiss than the first. 'You're awake,' he said solemnly. 'Trust me.'

'Yes, I . . . I . . .' She drew in her breath and then let it out. 'When I woke up and you weren't here, I . . . I . . .'

Blake smiled. 'You what?' he asked softly, cupping her face in his hands.

Elena swallowed hard. 'I . . . I . . .'

'Were you upset?'

She nodded. 'Yes,' she said finally.

He smiled again. 'Tell me why.'

'Tell you...? Well, because I...because I...'

'Because you love me,' he said.

Her eyes widened. 'No, I don't, I...'

Blake lifted her face to his. 'Don't lie to me,' he said firmly. 'Wives should never lie to their husbands.'

Her eyes closed. 'Please don't tease me,' she whispered. 'We're not married any more. You know that. You came all this way to make sure of that. Those annulment papers...'

'Yeah,' he said thoughtfully, 'I know. Signing them seemed like the right thing—I figured you wanted out and I owed it to you.'

'*I* wanted out?'

He shrugged. 'But after I put them in the mail, I got to thinking.' His eyes flickered over her. 'I began to wonder if I'd been right about you all along. So I decided to come to Miami and find out.' His lips curved in a quick smile. 'And I did.'

Elena looked at him blankly. 'You did what? Blake, I don't know what you're talking about. You have those papers right in your pocket. You...'

He laughed softly. 'Hold out your hand,' he said.

Her lashes lifted and she frowned. 'What?'

'Hold out your hand,' he repeated patiently.

'Blake, what's this all about? I...' Blake reached into his jacket pocket and Elena stared into her upturned palm as he filled it with tiny bits of charred paper. 'What is this stuff?' she demanded.

'Our annulment papers,' he said smugly. Her bewildered eyes met his and he shrugged his shoulders. 'I know I should have invited you to the ceremony, but...'

Elena looked at him and shook her head. 'Have you gone crazy, Rogan? What are you talking about? How could you have burned those papers? Now we'll have to start from scratch. We...'

'No annulment.'

Her heart began to race. 'What?'

Blake shrugged. 'No annulment,' he said as he stood up. 'Would you like me to spell it out? Capital "n", small "o". Space. Small "a"...'

'Blake, for God's sake—what do you mean, no annulment? That's why you came here, remember? To make sure it had gone through.'

He pulled off his jacket and tossed it aside. 'We're going to have to do something about this problem of yours, Princess. No matter how many times I tell you to pay attention, you just don't do it. I didn't come here for the annulment,' he said while he unbuttoned his shirt. 'I came for the annulment papers.' He nodded to the bits of paper she still held in her hand and smiled. 'And I sure as hell got 'em.'

Elena looked from her hand to Blake's face. 'I don't understand this at all,' she said slowly.

He sighed as he sat down beside her. 'OK, I'll explain, Princess. Come here,' he said, and before she could protest, he nestled her against him. 'I won't agree to an annulment,' he said, watching her carefully. 'You're going to remain Mrs Blake Rogan.'

There was a wild pounding behind her ribs. Surely, her heart was going to leap from her chest. But when she spoke, Elena's voice was calm.

'I am?'

His arm tightened around her. 'We've gone past the annulment stage, Princess. We've consummated our marriage any number of times.'

'Blake,' she said, 'I don't know what you're up to, but...'

'I love you, Elena.'

Her heart turned over. 'What?' she whispered.

Blake smiled into her eyes. 'I love you,' he said. 'Even though you're the most contrary woman I've ever met.'

'I'm not,' she said quickly, and he laughed.

'See what I mean? But you'll learn, Princess. In fact,' he said teasingly, 'we'll keep the words "to obey" in the marriage ceremony. I know it's fashionable to leave them out today, but...'

Elena put her hand across his mouth. 'What marriage ceremony? You just said we were still married, and now...'

'Yes, well, better safe than sorry. That's what my mother always says, anyway. So, just in case there's any question about our marriage, we'll do it again.' He brushed a kiss across her lips. 'Do you think your father would come to Philadelphia for the wedding? We'll have to be there for a couple of months so my father can brief me before I take over the European operations of the firm.'

'Blake,' she said carefully, 'I don't know what you're talking about. What firm?'

'Rogan International. I promised my father I'd become a director of the European branch. I can't wait to show you Paris in the spring and London at Christmas and...'

Elena let out her breath. 'Blake,' she said slowly, her eyes searching his face. 'Are you really saying...are you telling me you...you love me?'

He smiled tenderly. 'Yes, Princess. I love you with all my heart.' He kissed her and put his hand to her cheek. 'I'll always love you, Elena.'

Tears of happiness filled her eyes. She clasped his hand and pressed her lips to his palm.

'I'm not dreaming?' Blake shook his head and she laughed softly. 'Then maybe you'd better start at the beginning and explain.'

His smile faded. 'You won't like the beginning.'

'You mean, my father's role in all this,' she said slowly, and he nodded.

'I'm afraid so, Princess. Your father and I met for the first time a few days after you and I had our little encounter in the Santa Rosa market. I was interested in some mining property—well, never mind the business details.' Blake took a deep breath and let it out slowly. 'I was surprised when he invited me to your birthday party. Once I reached the ranch, he took me into his study. He said he'd heard I had a reputation as a man who could handle himself in a tight spot, and he wanted to ask a favour of me. He told me he was arranging for you to leave San Felipe. But he was afraid things were coming to a head more quickly than anyone had expected. He asked if I'd agree to get you out of the country if there was trouble.'

Elena looked at him. 'He didn't ask you to marry me?'

'No, Princess, not then.' Blake's arm tightened around her. 'I said I would help him. Oh, I refused at first—but eventually, I let him talk me into it.' He tilted her face to his and kissed her. 'I told myself it was the decent thing to do, but hell, I have to admit I was intrigued with the idea. I'd had trouble getting you out of my mind since the day we'd met. I thought you were spoiled and headstrong—but there was something about you I just couldn't forget.'

Elena shook her head. 'But I don't understand, Blake. When did he ask you to marry me? And why? If you'd already agreed to help...'

'Your father phoned me that same night. It was right after the fighting started. He was afraid they wouldn't let you leave the country under your own name and with your own papers. And that's when he said...'

'I know what he said,' she whispered. 'He said he'd pay you to make me your wife.'

Blake sighed. 'No, not quite, Princess. This is the part you're not going to like. He said I'd either marry you or he'd see to it that I'd rot inside a San Felipian jail.'

'No,' she said emphatically, 'no, not my father! His honour is his life. He . . .'

'Yes, that's what he said,' Blake murmured, settling back into the sofa and drawing her head to his shoulder. 'But he also said that when the safety of his daughter was at stake, he had no choice.'

Elena's voice was a whisper. 'Poor Papa. He said his arrangement with you had cost him a great deal, but I didn't understand.'

'He loves you very much, Elena.'

She nodded. 'Yes,' she said softly, 'yes, he does. I . . . I don't think I ever realised just how much.' She looked up and her eyes searched his. 'And you never told me the truth. You let me say all those terrible things to you about the money he'd paid you . . .'

Blake pressed his lips to her hair. 'Yeah. At first, I promised myself I'd tell you the truth when you least expected it and repay you for all the things you'd said about me. But after a while, when I began to know the real you—hell, Princess, I just couldn't do it.'

Elena shuddered. 'You must hate my father for what he did to you.'

Blake shook his head. 'No, I don't hate him. I'd do whatever had to be done to protect you, too, Princess. Besides,' he said with a smile, 'if he hadn't forced us into marriage, we might never have found each other again after that day in the market.' He put his finger to the tip of her nose. 'You thought I was one step up from a tramp.'

A smile tilted at her lips. 'Not a tramp,' she said. 'A bandit. Handsome, exciting...'

'...and dirty. I'd just spent a week in the interior, checking out some mining claims. I was hot, sweaty—and then I saw you, Elena, so cool and beautiful and...' Suddenly, his hands closed on her shoulders and he held her from him. 'You still haven't said you love me.' His eyes, as blue as the sea, blazed into hers. 'Dammit, I know you do. I thought so that last night in the cave, but...'

'Then why did you act as you did the next morning?' she whispered. 'If you loved me—if you thought I loved you... why did you let me think you were afraid I might try and trap you into staying married to me?'

Blake's face twisted in pain. 'Jesus, is that what you...?' He pulled her to him and kissed her until she was breathless. 'I thought I made it all so clear, love. Hell, you were young and innocent. First, you'd been forced into marriage and then I—I seduced you...'

Elena shook her head. 'I wanted you to make love to me, Blake,' she murmured. 'I was afraid to admit it, even to myself, but...'

'Yes, I kept telling myself that the next morning, when I woke up feeling guilty as hell. When I started to apologise for what had happened, I had some crazy hope you'd throw your arms around my neck and tell me you loved me.' His face darkened. 'But you didn't. You said it had been a mistake, that it hadn't been as special to you as it was to me, and I damned near died, Elena, I...'

'Hush,' she said fiercely. She put her hands on either side of his head and looked into his eyes. 'I love you, Blake Rogan,' she said. 'Do you hear me? I love you, I...'

He caught her to him in a passionate kiss. When they finally broke apart, he grinned.

'I suppose I should feel sorry for poor Jeremy,' he said. 'But I don't. Hell, any man who'd let you go off alone to San Felipe...' His voice dropped to a husky whisper. 'Any man who'd never taken you in his arms and made love to you...'

Elena sighed. 'Jeremy's my boss and a good friend, but he was never anything more. I just told you he was my fiancé because I thought...I suppose I thought it would protect me.'

He laughed softly. 'But it didn't work.'

'Nothing would have worked,' she said simply, looking deep into his eyes, 'not once I'd fallen in love with you.' She smiled and kissed him. 'I just wish I knew exactly who you are. I mean, one second you're Blake Rogan, adventurer, and the next you're the new director of the European branch...'

'Does it matter?'

'No,' she said so quickly that they both laughed. 'No, not a bit. I'd go with you to Belize or Somalia or,' she smiled wickedly, 'or even Philadelphia.'

He grinned. 'OK, the life story of Blake Rogan, in one quick paragraph. My old man founded Rogan International before I was born. We invest in damned near anything that has value, worldwide—which is what saved my wandering soul. You see, when I finished college, my father wanted me to become his right-hand man. But I had no desire to bury myself in an office— not then, anyway. Hell, I was twenty-one and there was a whole world to see.'

Elena looked up at him. 'That was what you meant when you said he'd found you a job and you turned it down?'

Blake nodded. 'So he and my mother talked it over and decided that I could learn the business just as well if I went into the field and searched out investment opportunities. They knew I'd never be happy unless I got the adventure bug out of my system.'

'And have you? I . . . I don't want you to change, just for me, Blake. I . . .'

He put his hand beneath her chin and lifted her face to his. 'You're the next adventure, Princess,' he said. 'You—and maybe, some day, a little girl who's the image of her beautiful mother.'

Elena smiled happily. 'She'll need a brother, of course.'

He laughed softly. 'Of course.' He kissed her tenderly and then he drew back and looked at her. 'Anything else, Princess?'

She looked at him thoughtfully. 'So your parents didn't throw you out, hmm? They're not the cold, cruel people I imagined they were?'

He grinned. 'You're gonna love 'em both, Princess. They. . . Hey!' he said indignantly, as she poked him in the ribs. 'What was that for?'

'For letting me think you'd been tossed out into the world. That was rotten!'

'So was letting me think you were in love with old Jeremy,' Blake growled, drawing her down to lie beside him on the couch.

'I was simply safeguarding my virtue, *señor*,' Elena said solemnly as she snuggled herself more closely against him. 'I'm an Esteban, after all. I was a very properly raised *señorita*. I knew nothing about such things.'

Blake chuckled. 'What things?'

'The things you wanted to show me, Señor Rogan.'

'Uh huh,' he murmured, and he bit her gently on the neck. 'But you're a quick learner, Princess.'

'That's the Kelly part,' she said. 'My mother always thought girls should learn as much as they were able.'

'Which is very good news, Mrs Rogan,' Blake whispered. 'You see, I still have an awful lot to teach you.'

His arms closed around her and he rolled her beneath him. 'And I thought, what the heck, this damned couch is too narrow to sleep on anyway, so...' He looked down at her and frowned. 'What are you smiling at, *señora*?' he demanded with mock ferocity. 'This isn't a joking matter.'

Elena laughed softly. 'Remind me to tell you all about Margarita some time,' she whispered. Blake moved above her and her arms rose and wound around his neck. 'Some time,' she said with a sigh, 'but definitely not now.'

Harlequin Presents

Coming Next Month

1199 THE ALOHA BRIDE Emma Darcy
Robyn is at a low point in her life and is determined not to be hurt again Then she meets Julian Lassiter Somehow she finds herself wanting to solve Julian's problems in a way that is not only reckless but is positively dangerous!

1200 FANTASY LOVER Sally Heywood
Torrin Anthony's arrival in Merril's life is unwanted and upsetting, for this shallow, artificial actor reminds her of Azur—the heroic rebel sympathizer who'd rescued her from cross fire in the Middle East. Could she possibly be mixing fantasy with reality?

1201 WITHOUT TRUST Penny Jordan
Lark Cummings, on trial for crimes she's innocent of, hasn't a chance when she is faced with James Wolfe's relentless prosecution. Then the case is inexplicably dropped. She wants to hate this formidable man, but finds it impossible when fate brings him back into her life!

1202 DESPERATION Charlotte Lamb
Megan accepts a year apart from her newfound love, Devlin Hurst—she'll wait for him. Yet when her life turns upside down just hours after his departure, she knows she must break their pact. Only she has to lie to do it.

1203 TAKE AWAY THE PRIDE Emma Richmond
Toby lies about her qualifications to become secretary to powerful Marcus du Mann—and is a disaster But when Marcus gets stuck with his baby nephew, Toby is put in charge. And she's coping well—until Marcus decides to move in and help

1204 TOKYO TRYST Kay Thorpe
Two years ago, Alex walked out on Greg Wilde when she discovered he was unfaithful Now they're on the same work assignment in Japan. Despite Greg's obvious interest in the beautiful Yuki, Alex finds herself falling in love with him all over again!

1205 IMPULSIVE GAMBLE Lynn Turner
Free-lance journalist Abbie desperately wants a story on reclusive engineer-inventor Malacchi Garrett. Then she discovers the only way to get close to him is by living a lie. But how can she lie to the man she's falling in love with?

1206 NO GENTLE LOVING Sara Wood
Hostile suspicion from wealthy Dimitri Kastelli meets Helen in Crete, where she's come to find out about the mother she never knew What grudge could he hold against a long-dead peasant woman? And how would he react if he learned who Helen is?

Available in September wherever paperback books are sold, or through Harlequin Reader Service:

In the U.S.
901 Fuhrmann Blvd.
P.O. Box 1397
Buffalo, N.Y 14240-1397

In Canada
P.O Box 603
Fort Erie, Ontario
L2A 5X3

Harlequin American Romance®

Gull Cottage

The sun, the surf, the sand...

One relaxing month by the sea was all Zoe, Diana and Gracie ever expected from their four-week stay at Gull Cottage, the luxurious East Hampton mansion. They never thought that what they found at the beach would change their lives forever.

Join Zoe, Diana and Gracie for the summer of their lives. Don't miss the GULL COTTAGE trilogy in Harlequin American Romance: #301 CHARMED CIRCLE by Robin Francis (July 1989); #305 MOTHER KNOWS BEST by Barbara Bretton (August 1989); and #309 SAVING GRACE by Anne McAllister (September 1989).

GULL COTTAGE—because one month can be the start of forever...

SWEEPSTAKES RULES & REGULATIONS

NO PURCHASE NECESSARY TO ENTER OR RECEIVE A PRIZE

1. To enter and join the Reader Service, check off the "YES" box on your Sweepstakes Entry Form and return to Harlequin Reader Service. If you do not wish to join the Reader Service but wish to enter the Sweepstakes only, check off the "NO" box on your Sweepstakes Entry Form. Incomplete and/or inaccurate entries are ineligible for that section or sections(s) of prizes. Not responsible for mutilated or unreadable entries or inadvertent printing errors. Mechanically reproduced entries are null and void. Be sure to also qualify for the Bonus Sweepstakes. See rule #3 on how to enter.

2. Either way, your unique Sweepstakes number will be compared against the list of winning numbers generated at random by the computer. In the event that all prizes are not claimed, random drawings will be held from all entries received from all presentations to award all unclaimed prizes. All cash prizes are payable in U.S. funds. This is in addition to any free, surprise or mystery gifts that might be offered. The following prizes are offered: *Grand Prize (1) $1,000,000 Annuity; First Prize (1) $35,000; Second Prize (1) $10,000; Third Prize (3) $5,000; Fourth Prize (10) $1,000; Fifth Prize (25) $500; Sixth Prize (5,000) $5.
   * This Sweepstakes contains a Grand Prize offering of a $1,000,000 annuity. Winner may elect to receive $25,000 a year for 40 years without interest; totalling $1,000,000 or $350,000 in one cash payment. Entrants may cancel Reader Service at any time without cost or obligation to buy.

3. Extra Bonus Prize: This presentation offers two extra bonus prizes valued at $30,000 each to be awarded in a random drawing from all entries received. To qualify, scratch off the silver on your Lucky Keys. If the registration numbers match, you are eligible for the prize offering.

4. Versions of this Sweepstakes with different graphics will be offered in other mailings or at retail outlets by Torstar Corp. and its affiliates. This promotion is being conducted under the supervision of Marden-Kane, Inc., an independent judging organization. By entering this Sweepstakes, each entrant accepts and agrees to be bound by these rules and the decisions of the judges, which shall be final and binding. Odds of winning in the random drawing are dependent upon the total number of entries received. Taxes, if any, are the sole responsibility of the winners. Prizes are nontransferable. All entries must be received by March 31, 1990. The drawing will take place on or about April 30, 1990 at the offices of Marden-Kane, Inc., Lake Success, N.Y.

5. This offer is open to residents of the U.S., United Kingdom and Canada, 18 years or older, except employees of Torstar Corp., its affiliates, subsidiaries, Marden-Kane and all other agencies and persons connected with conducting this Sweepstakes. All Federal, State and local laws apply. Void wherever prohibited or restricted by law.

6. Winners will be notified by mail and may be required to execute an affidavit of eligibility and release, which must be returned within 14 days after notification. Canadian winners will be required to answer a skill-testing question. Winners consent to the use of their name, photograph and/or likeness for advertising and publicity in conjunction with this or similar promotions, without additional compensation.

7. For a list of our most current major prize winners, send a stamped, self-addressed envelope to: Winners List, c/o Marden-Kane, Inc., P.O. Box 701, Sayreville, N.J. 08871.

If Sweepstakes entry form is missing, please print your name and address on a 3" × 5" piece of plain paper and send to:

In the U.S.	In Canada
Sweepstakes Entry	Sweepstakes Entry
901 Fuhrmann Blvd.	P.O. Box 609
P.O. Box 1867	Fort Erie, Ontario
Buffalo, NY 14269-1867	L2A 5X3